THE
COMIC
CAFé

Roger
Stevens

F

FRANCES LINCOLN
CHILDREN'S BOOKS

First published in Great Britain and the USA in 2012 by
Frances Lincoln Children's Books, 4 Torriano Mews,
Torriano Avenue, London NW5 2RZ
www.franceslincoln.com

A catalogue record for this book is available from
the British Library.

ISBN: 978-1- 84780-270-5

Set in Palatino

Printed in Croydon, Surrey, UK
by CPI Bookmarque Ltd. in February 2012

1 3 5 7 9 8 6 4 2

For Lily, Ruby, Merlin and Sam

1
Ghost

S H E E E E A A A A A K K K K K ! ! ! !
SHEEEEAAAAAKKKKK!!!!

Vampyre's cry echoed through the lonely hills and valleys. The great bat-like creature drifted lower. The light of the gibbous moon glinted on its leathery body and wings. Its moon-shadow drifted slowly across the spiky trees and barren ground. Owls and other night dwellers hid from its view. It was seeking its master. And heading my way.

With a start I opened my eyes. Darkness. I could see only darkness.

I felt for the clock and peered at the luminous hands, trying to see the time. It looked like a quarter past twelve. No, it was three o'clock. I'd only been asleep for two hours. And I'd been dreaming of a favourite character of mine – Vampyre.

Sheeeaaakkkk! SHEEEAAAKKKK!!!

But the cry wasn't a dream. It was real, and coming from somewhere in the house. A chill ran through me, as though someone had opened a door and let a cold wind in, and I shivered.

I hid beneath the duvet. There it was again. But now it sounded more like a voice. Far away, but at the same time very close. I know that's impossible, but that's what it was like. Like the voices you hear in the horror films we're not supposed to watch. I strained to hear what the voice was saying.

Help me. Help. Help. Help. Help!

In the distance I could hear waves crashing on the beach, and all around the old house the wind groaning and rattling the windows.

Help me. Help. Help. Help. Help!

I got up, pulled on my boxer shorts and crept out onto the landing. I could hear Elizabeth snoring softly. She said she didn't snore but we all knew she did. No sound came from Jaz's or Briony's rooms.

I could feel some sort of unearthly presence nearby. Like a ghost, or unwelcome spirit. I looked up. Here at the top of the house there was a trapdoor in the ceiling. Was the noise coming from there? Was there something in the loft? A ghoul, crouching above the door ready to drop on an unsuspecting victim? A hungry ghoul with red eyes and sharp teeth?

Getting out of bed had been a bad idea. I should simply have buried my head under the duvet and gone back to sleep.

There was the weird moaning voice again, like a creature in pain. *Help me. Help me. Help me, Wilf!*

Did it say my name? I shuddered. I needed the loo. I crept down the stairs to the first landing. I listened at my youngest sister, Sammi's door. I could hear her soft breathing. Next to her room was Mum and Dad's. What if there was someone in there? An intruder? A burglar? I listened at their door. I could hear the sound again, but now it seemed to be coming from the café below.

I made my way slowly down the stairs to the ground floor, my bare feet treading lightly on the dusty bare wood. The stairs creaked. Before me was the door to the cellar. It was locked. In the cellar lived the Gargoyle – a gruesome creature, with wild eyes and green skin, half man, half giant bat, manacled to the wall with rusty iron chains. The Gargoyle had once been Lord of the Skies of the Underworlds, holding dominion over all foul creatures that flew. Not one of us had yet dared to enter the cellar and confront the monster.

I crept past the door and peered into the gloomy café. A glimmer of light from the road tried to illuminate the room, but it was hopeless. There was no way for light to penetrate the thick, sludgy layers of grime on the windows, the salt, the dirt from passing cars and the seagull poo.

SHEEEEAAAAAKKKKK!!!!

A huge, white, ghostly shape ran towards me. My heart leapt to my mouth and I felt dizzy. I felt its body push against me. I felt its warm fur brush me. It hissed.

I let out a loud sigh of relief. It was only Killer – the enormous white cat we'd inherited with the building. Killer was no ghost – he was very real. He looked up at me, growled quietly and, back arched, crept stealthily back into the room, as though he, too, could sense the ghost's presence and was determined to put an end to its misery.

I turned on the light. The large room was a tip. Broken chairs and rickety tables were strewn about the place. Cobwebs hung from the ceiling beams.

There was a smell of decay, soot and stale food. Had the ghostly noises stopped? No . . . they were coming from upstairs again.

Help! Help me, Wilf. Wilf! Wilf!

I turned the light off, left Killer crouched in the café's darkness and retraced my steps. I paused on the first landing and listened again at my parents' door. The sound was coming from their room. I could feel my heart thudding and my hands were damp. I opened the door slowly and peered in. The door creaked, but the voice stopped and I could see that there was no ghost there.

The room was lit by moonlight. There was Mum and Dad's unslept-in bed, the duvet piled up in a big, untidy heap where they'd left it. I peered hard at the shadowy corners, half-expecting something to leap out at me from behind the big cardboard boxes still waiting to be unpacked after the move. I felt suddenly tearful and I wondered where Mum and Dad were right now.

The ghostly voice stopped.

Silence.

Back in the warmth of my bed, I wondered if the house really was haunted. But I had no idea then, as I lay in the dark, listening to the distant waves and the wind in the rafters, that a greater mystery was waiting to be solved. Far more dangerous and scary than ghostly noises in the night.

Eventually I must have dozed off.

Vampyre was seeking its master – the Gargoyle. Vampyre

drifted through the dark shadows below the blue and silver cloud towards the tall stone chimneys of the ancient, crumbling mansion. In the cellar, the Gargoyle moved nervously to and fro, sensing Vampyre's arrival. Dark, formless beings met in the dim café, sipping black coffee and nibbling black pudding, waiting for the Gargoyle's release.

2
A Fond Farewell
to Father

"Let's get this straight," I said. "You think we'd be better off without you? You really and truly think that we'd be better off without a father?"

"Well . . . yes . . . sort of . . . no . . . um. . . ."

Dad absent-mindedly rubbed a little hole in the condensation on the café window with his plastic spoon and peered through. I rubbed a little hole with my finger and peered too. Outside, a wet and bedraggled holidaymaker was chasing a giant yellow-and-green blow-up dinosaur across the road. A Force 10 gale was hurling it towards the beach.

"Look, Wilf," Dad went on, "all I'm saying is this. Me and Mum argue all the time. We shout. We fight. We're at it hammer and tongs all day and all night. And it's my fault. I know it is. I shouldn't have moved us all here. I shouldn't have taken you away from all your mates."

Well, he was right there. I thought about Josh and

wondered what he was doing now. Probably sitting in a café with his dad, too. But on holiday in Spain, in the blazing sunshine, sipping an ice-cold Coke.

I peered through the window again. The dinosaur had snagged itself on an abandoned ice-cream van and the holidaymaker had nearly caught up with it.

"I shouldn't have brought you to this miserable town," Dad said. "It's a dump."

"It's not a dump. It's the seaside," I said. "It's great. We love the seaside. It's not stopped raining since we got here but that's not your fault, is it?"

Dad sighed and started searching the tabletop for something, moving the plastic salt and pepper pots and nudging his cup and saucer to one side. He lifted up the little vase of droopy plastic primroses and put it down again. He obviously couldn't find what he was looking for. He sighed again, pulled out a pen from his top pocket and used it to stir his tea.

I looked around. The only other customers were a wet family huddled round a table near the door. Their plastic raincoats were dripping on to the floor and the drips had formed a small lake. They were all silent except for the toddler in the pushchair, who was whimpering quietly.

This place wasn't exactly doing a roaring trade. Not

for the first time, I wondered whether it had been such a good idea to buy a café in a place like this. Because that was why we'd moved here. We'd bought a derelict café, or "restaurant", as dad liked to call it, and we were going to do it up and make our fortunes.

"I'll only be gone for a few weeks," Dad said. "Maybe a couple of months. Just to give your mum some space. To give her a break. I'm just a dead weight."

"You're not," I said.

"I am. I'm a cannonball hanging round her neck, dragging her down. Or a bag of potatoes. Something heavy, anyway."

"You're not a bag of potatoes."

"I am," Dad said gloomily. "A bag of spuds. A bag of Maris Piper. Going green. Useless."

"You're not going green," I said. "And you're not useless. You repaired that clock."

"That was years ago. Anyway, I didn't mend it. All I did was change the battery. Look, I've made up my mind. Mum will be a lot happier with me gone."

"She won't," I said. But I knew that she probably would. I'm sure they did love one another, really. But they weren't getting on at the moment. And the move had definitely made things worse between them.

"Tell your sisters I love them. And it's not their fault."

"OK."

"And give this to Mum for me." He produced a creased brown envelope from his inside pocket.

"OK," I said.

"Wilf, don't lose it."

There was a loud *clump* from outside, followed by the tinkle of breaking glass. We both cleared new holes in the misted-up window and peered out.

"It's a motorbike," I said. "A big one with those high chrome handles. Dead flashy."

"Nice," Dad said. "I've always fancied getting a motorbike. A Harley-Davidson. A Sportster."

"It's had a bit of an accident. Bashed into a car."

"Someone's holiday spoiled. That's all you need on your holiday – paying out for car repairs."

"It's our car," I said.

Dad sighed an even bigger sigh than normal and pulled himself to his feet. We made our way out, negotiating the whimpering toddler in the pushchair and the wet family reading holiday brochures for Majorca. We waded through the small lake to the door.

Outside, the wind had eased a little and the

downpour was now just heavy rain. I looked up. Above us, a flock of seagulls were attacking the holidaymaker. She was hanging from the big blow-up dinosaur. The dinosaur was caught in the wind, flying across the sky, probably heading towards Paris. I wondered whether the woman had her passport.

The motorbike had hit the back of the car and broken the lights.

"Don't worry," Dad said. "I'll sort this out." He pulled me to him and gave me a clumsy hug. I spotted the plastic spoon in his top pocket, but decided not to tell him. He'd probably left his pen in the sugar.

"You get off home," he said. "And give Mum the letter. I'll see you soon. Just a couple of weeks."

At the corner I turned back. Dad was talking to the owner of the motorbike, a massive, bearded biker in a studded leather jacket. A small crowd clutching inside-out umbrellas had gathered to watch. This was obviously what counted as entertainment in this town. Soon someone would be selling programmes.

I turned the corner and headed for home.

3
Missing Mother
Already

When I got back I couldn't find Mum, so I sat in my bedroom and looked at the picture of my family on the computer screen. It was stuck to the screen with sticky tape. I'd inherited the computer from Mum and Dad, who'd bought a laptop when we moved. They'd bought a new computer because their old PC was running slow. Now it had stopped running altogether, had sat down for a rest and wasn't going to get up again for anyone, especially me.

I'd taken the photo on my camera before Dad borrowed it and dropped it in the sea. It wasn't his fault, though – he'd been startled by a curious crab. Well, he thought it was a crab. It was actually a piece of seaweed caught between his toes.

The photo showed Mum and Dad smiling. I wondered why people always smiled in photos. It could be the worst holiday ever – Mum stung by jellyfish, Dad sunburnt to a crisp, the credit cards stolen, the car swallowed by a giant inflatable dinosaur – but everyone would still have big cheesy grins on their faces.

I'd taken the photo last year on the beach in the south of France. And it had been a good holiday, for once. Mum and Dad looked happy and I do believe they were. And there were my four sisters – Elizabeth, Jaz, Briony and Sammi – all cheerful and smiling and not arguing at all.

I'm the oldest. Elizabeth is one year younger than me, although she's bigger than I am. Dad says she's "solid". She gets upset about this because of her size, but Dad means she's reliable. Dad should think before he speaks. As Mum says, Before using mouth, engage brain.

Jaz is a year younger. She's boy crazy. All she does is play with make-up and listen to pop music. She takes after Mum. (I don't mean Mum is boy crazy!) Jaz is full of energy, whizzing about from one project to the next. And she's thin like Mum, too. She can eat bucketfuls of food and never gets fat.

Then there's brainy Briony. Her hair's black and she wears black clothes. She's going to be a Goth when she grows up, I think. She's very quiet – in fact, she didn't speak until she was nearly five and everyone was really worried. The first words she said were to her teacher: "Can I have a more grown-up book, please?" When asked why she'd taken so long to talk, she said she hadn't had anything interesting to say.

And finally there's Sammi, the youngest, the baby of the family. Mum says she still has her puppy fat.

There was a knock on the door and Elizabeth came in. Her eyes were red and I surmised she'd been crying. (I like trying out interesting words.)

"Have you been crying?" I asked her. She nodded. "I surmised as much," I said.

She gathered up the comics spread all over the bed and lumped them on top of a box in the corner. A couple of my favourite Dark Avengers slid off the heap and joined the general mess on the floor. Then she moved the football cards that I'd been sorting and shoved aside a couple of my sketchbooks and some drawings I'd been working on.

"Budge up," she told Killer.

Killer is rather striking. His fur is pure white. You could say he was beautiful. But with his size and his swagger and his yellowy-green stare, you'd be more likely to say he was scary. He's the feline equivalent of Arnold Schwarzenegger in a bad mood. The only person he likes is Sammi. He lets her pick him up and make a fuss of him as if he was a regular cat. But he won't let anyone else near him. Sammi calls him Kevin. We call him Killer.

Killer stared back at Elizabeth. He didn't move. Elizabeth sat down gingerly next to him, careful not to make any sudden movements. Between them, they took up the entire bed. Actually, that's not really true. I must try and be nicer about my sister. She's not really fat. As Mum says, she's just big-boned.

"It's not fair," Elizabeth said.

"Oh, I don't know," I said. "I don't mind the cat sitting there. And there's room for the two of you. Well, almost."

"I don't mean that. I mean, life isn't fair." A tear gathered in the corner of her eye and began to creep down the side of her nose. "I've some bad news. . ." The tear gathered speed and ran around the side of her mouth before sprinting down her chin and leaping into space. "We're a one-parent family now, Wilf."

So she knew. I didn't think Dad had told anyone else.

"I know," I said. I sat next to her and put my arm around her in a huggy, older-brother sort of way.

"Thanks." She sniffed, and gave me half a smile.

I moved back to my computer chair. I knew Elizabeth would like a real hug. I just didn't want her to think

I might be making a habit of it. But it *was* a bit sad, Dad going off like that.

"Don't worry," I said. "It'll be fine. Mum and Dad do fight a lot. But at least it means there'll be some peace and quiet for a few weeks."

"I suppose so. But how will Dad cope? He's so hopeless."

"No, he's not," I said.

"He can't even organise his own breakfast. Mum has to show him where the Munchy Malcolms are every morning. And pour the milk on for him. And make sure he uses sugar, not salt."

"Yeah, that was funny, though, wasn't it?" I said.

"We'll just have to be patient with him, like Mum is," Elizabeth went on, "and help him."

"I guess so," I said. Then I thought . . . hang on a minute! How could we help him if he wasn't here?

"We can work out some sort of rota," Elizabeth went on.

"What are you talking about?"

"A rota." Elizabeth sighed. "You know, work out all the chores. I'll do the ironing. I quite like that. You can wash up. Mum said she'd be back in time for the start of school. So we've only got to cope for four weeks without her."

"Mum said? What do you mean?"

"I thought you knew. You said you knew. Mum's gone away for the summer. She's leaving Dad in charge."

"Oh dear," I said. "Oh dear."

How could this have happened? Not just Dad. Now Mum had gone as well! I got up and picked my way across the room and looked out of the window at the rain. Down below, a fat rat was examining the rubbish that littered the small backyard.

"Elizabeth, I've got some news, too," I said. . .

4
Heartbreak Hotel

Our move to the seaside had been a quick one. One minute we were all squeezed into a three-bedroomed semi in Slough; the next, we'd packed all our belongings into a large van and were heading for the coast. But this wasn't going to be a holiday.

Dad had had a good job working for a company that made packaged sandwiches. They bought white sliced bread and then froze it to take away all the taste and texture. Then they defrosted it, added thin slices of cheap, tasteless ham and soggy lettuce, and chilled the sandwiches to make them stay fresh longer and cause maximum discomfort to people with sensitive teeth. After they'd wrapped them in cardboard and plastic that was difficult to tear open, they sold them to corner shops and service stations. Yum, delicious. . .

Mum had worked for a plastics company making children's potties.

Then Dad was given the sack for loafing around and Mum was made redundant because the bottom had dropped out of the market. (That's Dad's brilliant joke, by the way.)

Mum got some redundancy money and they had some savings, and so they bought this place. It was Dad's dream – to retire to the seaside and open a little café.

The café's not little, though. It's massive. And it's very old. Everywhere is dark and gloomy and covered in cobwebs. It would make a great film set for a zombie movie or *The Curse of the Werewolf*. It's a total mess. The whole building's dilapidated.

It's in the old town – which sounds great, from a tourist's point of view – with narrow streets and 17th-century houses. But someone needs to spend money on the town before the whole lot falls down and a property developer turns it into a giant car park.

In our house, the café and the kitchen take up most of the ground floor. The café ceiling's quite high. There are old-fashioned beams, but the room has obviously been modernised some time in the past. Then there's a private dining-room painted bright green and the store room that will one day be an office. The building's been empty for five years. It was a squat for a while, the estate agent told us, and a kitchen fire had left a layer of soot over all the downstairs rooms.

The kitchen and the green room had been cleaned up a bit before we bought it, but the café itself was still covered in a thick, grimy layer of soot. And I don't know what the squatters had been doing in there, but most of the chairs were damaged. Needless to say, the property was very cheap – which was how we could afford to buy it. Not cheap enough, mind you. They must have seen Mum and Dad coming!

On the plus side, although the upstairs rooms are quite small, there are lots of them and so everyone gets to have a room of their own. Me, Elizabeth, Jaz and Briony on the top floor, then Sammi and Mum and Dad on the first floor.

There are stairs in the storeroom that go down to the dark, spooky cellar where the Gargoyle is chained up. Outside, there's a ramshackle shed in the yard. Gerald lives there. (That's the name Sammi's given the rat.)

We haven't actually been down into the cellar. Every time we turn the light on, the bulb blows. Dad said he'd take a look at the electrics himself, but Mum persuaded him not to. She wanted to call an electrician instead. Not that I'm keen to go down there. Who knows what spiders and other creepy-crawlies live there? Not that I'm scared of spiders, you understand – I think they're fascinating creatures.

Sammi says there's a ghost down there. She's convinced the house is haunted and has been since the day we arrived. I told her that the ghost wouldn't dare go down into the cellar on account of the Gargoyle.

Right now, everyone was assembled in the private dining-room, or the Pukey Green Room, as we call it – PGR for short. The walls really are a horrid colour. They make me feel seasick. We were sitting round the big oak table and Elizabeth and I were telling everyone the bad news. Although, curiously, nobody seemed to think the news was bad. And Jaz and Sammi weren't actually sitting. They were cavorting around the room whooping and cheering and punching the air. Jaz was yelling and chanting:

Hurrah! Hooray! Hurrah! Hooray!
We're going to have a holiday.
All be happy, don't be sad,
No more Mum and no more Dad.

And Sammi was joining in. She always did everything Jaz did. At last Elizabeth and I persuaded them to sit down and listen.

"They haven't left us for good, have they?" Jaz said.

"Well . . . no," Elizabeth said. "Mum said she'd

definitely be back before school starts – that's in about four weeks' time. She's just having a break."

"That's right," I said. "And Dad said he'd be away for a few weeks. It's just Mum and Dad having a holiday from one another."

"Well, there you are, then," said Jaz. "It's a holiday for us as well, isn't it? We can do what we like for a whole month. Play music really loud. Have a party. Invite hundreds of people. All our friends. I can wear my new top – the one with the silver butterflies. And my new silver boots."

"Except," Briony said, "all our friends live about sixty miles away. We don't know anyone here."

"Anyway," Jaz said, "that's not the point. The point is, we can do what we want. We can stay up till one in the morning. We can eat anything we want: Big Macs, Chinese takeaways . . . anything."

"Can I have a pizza?" Sammi asked.

"Of course you can," Jaz said. "Any flavour. What would you like? Syrup and chicken? Liver and beans? Shark and beetroot? Chocolate?"

"A chocolate pizza sounds good."

Jaz grinned. "How about frog and snot?"

Sammi pulled a face. Elizabeth gave Jaz a sort of disapproving-mother look. "I like Hawaiian," she said. "The one with the little bits of pineapple."

"You're so boring!" said Jaz.

"And we could have cream doughnuts for breakfast," Briony said.

"That's not really a good idea, though, is it?" Elizabeth said. "Some of us have to watch what we eat. We don't all look like rakes."

"Anyway," Briony said, "there's something you've all forgotten." And she paused, waiting for someone to ask what it was.

"Get on with it," Jaz said.

"If Mum and Dad have gone for, let us assume, an interval of four weeks, what, in the meantime, will we do for money? What will we live on? How will we buy food? Where will we get the money to buy it?"

"Trust you to think of that," Jaz said.

But Briony had a good point. We all looked at one another and thought hard.

"I've got seven pounds and twenty-three pence in my piggy bank," Sammi said. "And I've still got some Euros."

"Hmmm," Briony said. "That will be useful, little sister, but it's probably not going to be enough."

"How much is a pizza?" Sammi asked.

"Wait!" Briony said. "We're being stupid. We'll call

Dad and he'll come home. After all – he's not running away from us."

"Good plan," I said.

Briony reached for the phone and passed it to me and I called his number.

We waited expectantly. "Listen," Jaz said. We could hear a phone ringing upstairs. It was playing Elvis Presley's *Heartbreak Hotel*, Dad's favourite song.

"He's forgotten his phone," I said.

"What a prize dumbo," Jaz said.

"He's not a dumbo," I said. "At least he's *got* a mobile phone."

"Mum says they're bad for the brain," Elizabeth said. "There's no law that says you have to have one."

"You do have to have a brain," I said.

"Oh no," Jaz wailed. "We'll starve. What will we do? Oh dear, this is terrible."

"We could call Granny," Briony suggested.

"No way," we all said at the same time. Having Granny here would be a nightmare. Last time we stayed with her, we had to be in bed by seven. And up at six. Six in the morning? On a Saturday and Sunday? And she had no TV. She said it was an invention of the Devil. Granny was seriously weird.

"I'd rather eat my own arm than have Granny here," Jaz said.

"I do have another suggestion," Briony said.

"What's that?" Elizabeth asked.

"We could always use the Tesco account and order the food online. Mum used it last week. I helped her set it up, so I know the password."

"The Tesco account," I said. "That's brilliant, Briony. See? There's always an answer to a problem if you look hard enough."

"Hooray . . . chocolate pizza!" Sammi yelled.

"Yeah, but if Dad had remembered to take his phone. . ." Jaz began.

"But he didn't," I said. "Anyway. . ."

"Talking of Granny," Jaz said, "How about a game of Dracula?"

5
The Face at
the Window

*Vampyre sailed silently on the icy wind, nearer and nearer,
until at last it found the ancient building where its master
was held captive. It adjusted its black, leathery wings and
drifted down towards the building. Despite its great weight,
it landed lightly on the rooftop. Its bloodshot eyes peered
eagerly around. I am here at last, it thought. It stamped on
the fragile slate.*

Thunk!

And a second time.

Thunk!

And a third.

Thunk!

"Wilf!" Elizabeth prodded me. "There's someone at
the window."

"Sorry," I said. "I was miles away. I haven't woken
up properly yet."

A face was peering in through the grimy glass.

"We're closed!" Elizabeth called out.

The face continued to stare. The person knocked

again. I got up, went over to the window and peered through the grime. There stood a woman dressed in a long black raincoat, holding a big black umbrella.

"We're closed," I said loudly.

"Neighbour," she mouthed. "Can I come in?"

I turned to Elizabeth. "She says she's a neighbour. She wants to come in. I think it might be Mary Poppins."

"Tell her to come back in half an hour," Elizabeth said.

"Can you come back in half an hour?" I asked her through the glass. The neighbour nodded and went away.

"Come on," Elizabeth said. "Let's get dressed."

"I am dressed," I said.

"Well, then, you win first prize. Award yourself a coconut. We'll get the others up and dressed and then we'll see what our neighbour has to say."

"Good plan."

"I suppose getting the others up will be one of my jobs, then, as the oldest girl."

"Guess what? Guess what? Guess what?" Sammi came bounding into the room. "Guess what?"

"It's all a bad dream?" Elizabeth said. "Any moment we're going to wake up and we'll be back at our old house with all our friends – right?"

"And the sun will be shining," I added.

"Yeah," Elizabeth said, "and we've won the lottery."

"No," Sammi said.

"Have aliens landed, bringing peace on Earth?" I ventured.

Sammi shook her head.

"Has the Gargoyle in the cellar escaped?"

"No, no – don't be silly. Mum rang!"

"What?" Elizabeth said. "Wow! Fantastic!"

"What did she say? Is she on her way home?" I asked.

Sammi grinned. "She said she was well and she misses us already and she's in Spain staying with an old school friend she met . . . um . . . somewhere, and she hopes Dad's looking after us all right and he's coping . . . and we're to make sure he doesn't pour salt on his Munchy Malcolms . . . and she'll send us a postcard . . . and she sends her love and big huge hugs."

"But when's she coming home?" Elizabeth asked.

"Er, I'm not sure," Sammi said.

"Well, she must have said. What did she say when you told her about Dad?" I asked.

"What do you mean?"

"You know," Elizabeth said. "When she found out that Dad had gone, too. Didn't she say she'd come straight back?"

"Um . . . er. . ."

"Sammi," said Elizabeth, "you *did* tell Mum that Dad had gone, didn't you? You did explain that we are here on our own and that we have no money."

"I've got seven pounds, twenty-three pence in my piggy bank. And some Euros."

"Sammi! Did you tell her?"

Sammi looked guilty. "I think I forgot. It was too early. I had to get out of bed to answer the phone. And I was so excited to talk to her . . . I forgot."

"Sammi! How could you?" Elizabeth said. "Didn't Mum want to talk to any of us?"

"Yes, she did."

"Well?"

"I told her you were all still in bed and fast asleep."

"Oh, Sammi!" Elizabeth said.

Sammi burst into tears. "I'm sorry."

Elizabeth sighed, got up and gave her a big cuddle. "It's not your fault," she said. "But if Mum rings again, make sure she speaks to me or Wilf – OK?"

Sammi nodded. "OK. Who was that knocking?"

"Mary Poppins," I said. "She's coming back later."

"Really? Will she teach us how to fly?"

"It's not really Mary Poppins," Elizabeth told her.

"I'm not sure we should let her in, though," I said.

"She can take us up on to the roof to do a dance," said Sammi.

"What do you mean?" Elizabeth asked.

"You know, you jump around waving chimney brushes and clicking your heels."

"No," Elizabeth said, patiently. "I'm asking Wilf why he doesn't want to invite her in."

"We don't want neighbours snooping around, do we?" I said. "If anyone finds out we're here on our own, they'll have Social Services round and we'll be put into a home, or something. I don't think we're legal."

"Mum and Dad have only gone on holiday," Elizabeth said. "They *will* be coming back. Anyway, we haven't met anyone yet and we've been here a fortnight. Mary Poppins might be able to tell us something about this place and why it's been empty for so long. And we don't have to tell her anything about us. We'll just say Mum and Dad are out."

I sighed. "I think that if anyone finds out we're here on our own. . ."

"I'm going to get dressed and get the others up. You can put the kettle on." Elizabeth sounded reassuringly businesslike.

"You'll look stupid wearing a kettle," Sammi said.

That was another of Dad's brilliant jokes. Still, Elizabeth and I laughed, even though we'd heard it about ninety-three times before. I think young children have to be encouraged, don't you?

6
The Woman in Black

"Zis café," Mrs Herring said, "vas called Rubens' Rest. Rubens vas famous Flemish painter who lived four hundred years ago."

I knew that, being an artist myself. That's what I'm going to do: go to college and study art. We also knew that was the name of our restaurant. It was written in peeling paint over the door.

"Rubens' paintings vere full of life," Mrs Herring went on. "He vas one of first artists to start using paintbrush to paint actual drawings, rather than to just fill in outlines."

Briony and Jaz were still in bed. Elizabeth had tried her best to get them up. Sammi was still in her room getting dressed. It usually took her a couple of hours – without Mum here to chivvy her along, it would probably take all day. We were sitting round one of the sturdier tables in the café, one that didn't wobble, on chairs that still had backs and a full complement of legs. There was just me, Elizabeth and our slightly strange visitor.

She was no Mary Poppins, though. She reminded me more of an extra in a horror movie. She was dressed all in black and her face was very pale – probably due to spending her days in castle dungeons and only coming out at night. She was quite old – even older than Mum and Dad, I'd say.

Mrs Herring had hung her coat on the back of one of the sturdier chairs where it was dripping a little rainy puddle on to the floor. Killer was sitting next to the coat, eyeing it warily as though it was an unwelcome guest, an animal intruder that had to be guarded – or possibly attacked.

"Where are you from?" I asked her.

"You noticed my accent? I am from Poland. I came here as young voman viz my fazer. That vas long time ago."

"What do you do?" Elizabeth enquired.

"I'm retired. I vas estate agent."

"You didn't sell Mum and Dad this house, did you?" I asked, aghast.

"No, I didn't."

"Thank goodness for that," I said.

"Don't you like it? It's lovely building. It has lots of history."

"I'm sure," I said. "The London Dungeon has bags

of history, too, but I wouldn't want to live there." As I said this, I had a mental picture of Mrs Herring, a bunch of keys in her hand, unlocking a dank, dark and dismal cell somewhere beneath the streets of London.

Mrs Herring took a measured sip of tea. "Very nice tea. Did you make it?"

Elizabeth nodded.

"Von't your mum mind?"

"Eh? What do you mean?" Elizabeth said. "I often make the tea."

"Of course you do," Mrs Herring said. "No, I mean inviting stranger in. You have to be careful zese days. Shopping, is she?"

"Oh . . . yes," Elizabeth said.

"And your dad?"

"Oh . . . um. . ." Elizabeth and I looked at one another.

"You do have dad? Oh. I'm sorry. Is he . . . dead?"

"No, it's OK," I said. "Yes, we do have a dad. He's away on business." I changed the subject. "Did you come here, then, when the café was up and running?"

"Couple of times. It vas long time ago."

"Was it busy?" Here was a chance, I thought, to find out if there were ever any customers. I couldn't imagine it ever being full of people.

"Da . . . I mean . . . yes, I zink so. It vas lot brighter zen, of course. You could see pictures on valls, for one zing."

The walls were covered in a film of soot. But beneath it you could just about make out some shapes painted on to the plaster.

"What are they?" Elizabeth asked. "They look like animals of some kind. Giant pigs?"

"No, not pigs." Mrs Herring smiled.

"Was the last owner an artist, then?" I asked. I was wondering if perhaps he'd painted the walls himself. Maybe he was a fan of Rubens. But Mrs Herring didn't answer me. She finished her cup of tea and laid it carefully down on the table.

"So . . . your mozer and fazer aren't here."

"Not at this exact moment," I said. "As we explained. . ."

"Are you planning to reopen café?" she asked.

"Of course," Elizabeth replied. "Mum and Dad hope to have it ready for next spring. We're going to renovate it, get new tables and chairs."

"Ven café open, your parents vill be very busy. And now, getting ready to open, zey vill need cleaner."

"I suppose so," Elizabeth said.

"Zat's vhy I came round. I do cleaning. Pension not

35

enough to live on. Please could you tell zis to your mum? I vill clean house as well as café. Zis place is too big for zem to manage on zair own."

"Sammi, our youngest sister, thinks it's haunted." I don't know why I said this. Maybe because last night's ghostly encounter was still in my mind. I was expecting Mrs Herring to tell me that was nonsense. But she didn't.

"Vell," she said. "I don't vant to scare you, but. . ." She paused for effect and leant forward. "Have you been in cellar?"

"We don't go down there much because the light doesn't work," Elizabeth said. She failed to admit that none of us had been down there at all.

Mrs Herring lowered her voice. "I'm not surprised. Zey say zer vas terrible murder in zis house. A hundred years ago or more. In cellar! Can't you feel it down zer? A sort of cold presence?"

"I'm not sure," Elizabeth said.

"If I do your cleaning, nozing you could pay me vould get me down zere."

There was a long, eery silence.

Then a loud howl.

The chair with the coat on it toppled backwards and the coat began moving across the floor.

Mrs Herring gasped, leaping to her feet.

I jumped up. Killer was dragging the coat by its collar towards the kitchen. I jabbed the cat with my foot and he dropped the coat, spat at me and strode from the room.

Elizabeth picked up the coat and dusted it down. "Sorry," she said. "That was Killer. We inherited him with the property."

"Maybe you should disinherit him," Mrs Herring said coldly. "You von't have many customers if he tries to steal zeir coats." Mrs Herring took her coat from Elizabeth. "Never mind. No harm done. Look at time. I must be going. Tell your mozer I called."

"We vill . . . er, will," Elizabeth said.

We let Mrs Herring out and locked the door.

"There, there, poor Kevin. . ." It was Sammi's voice. She was standing in the doorway holding Killer in her arms. This was not easy, as the cat was nearly as big as she was. "Did that nasty Mary Poppins fwighten you? You poor lickle pussy cat. Come with me and I'll get you some lovely milk." And Sammi disappeared with Killer into the kitchen.

"That was good," Elizabeth said, "meeting someone from the locality. She seemed very nice."

"I'm not sure," I replied. "There was something odd about her. . ."

"She seemed friendly enough."

"I think it was her pale face and thin lips."

"You can't not like someone because they have thin lips."

"Or it could have been her Transylvanian accent."

"She's from Poland. Poland and Transylvania are two different places."

"And what about the long incisor teeth for sucking blood?"

Elizabeth shook her head.

"And the murder in the cellar? We'd better not tell Sammi."

"There are no such things as ghosts, though, are there?" Elizabeth pointed out.

"Anyway," I said, "she looks too smart to be a cleaner."

Elizabeth shrugged and gathered up the empty cups. "I wonder what kind of animals *are* painted on the walls?"

"Whatever they are," I said, "I pity whoever has to clean all the muck and grime off to find out."

7
Briony Surfaces

The bell rang for lunch. For a moment I thought that Mum was back. We'd found a big old-fashioned hand bell in the shed which I'd scraped the rust off and generally cleaned up. Mum always rings it to tell us when food is ready.

I was lying on my bed. I must have fallen asleep. The comic I'd been reading had slid on to the floor and fallen open at a rather beautifully rendered drawing of a ghoul. I looked at the clock. Nearly three o'clock. A late lunch, then.

I hadn't had a lot of sleep last night, with the ghost waking me from my Vampyre dream of chimneys and moonlight with its scary *Sheeeaaakkkk* cries.

And because Mum and Dad weren't there, we'd played Dracula until we went to bed after midnight. Dracula's a card game. You have three cards and you have to score thirty-one points. I've never worked out why it's called Dracula, though. Maybe it's because you have to *count* a lot. . .

Anyway, at the end of the evening I was fifty-three

buttons up. That's pretty good. We always play for buttons. We have a huge biscuit tinful that Mum has collected over the years. Briony, of course, ended up the overall winner. (That doesn't mean she won a pair of overalls.) Sammi came out ahead, too, mainly because my sisters felt sorry for her every time she lost and gave her buttons. Unadventurous Elizabeth came out evens and Jaz, as usual, lost everything. It was great staying up late. Today we were all a bit tired.

Elizabeth and Sammi were in the PGR. I could hear Jaz singing to herself in the kitchen. It was Amber Lite's latest.

My boyfriend is better than your boyfriend.
My boyfriend will be my friend
Until the end of time and then. . .

"Look!" Elizabeth handed me a postcard. "This might cheer you up." The card was from Dad. He must have posted it soon after he left. It was addressed to us and not to Mum. And it was amazing that it got here so quickly, or at all, since he'd forgotten to use a stamp. It said:

Hope you are all well. I've decided to go to France where

a friend of mine is doing some building work for a rock star. I can't remember his name but I'll let you know later. The rock star, that is. I can remember my friend's name. Anyway, he's very famous. (Not my friend – the rock star.) So I'll be earning for a few weeks, at least. Tell Mum I'll send her some more money as soon as I can. Keep smiling. Lots of love and great big kisses – Dad.

"Well," I said, "That's good, then."

"I had to give the postman a pound, plus the cost of a stamp."

"Still no way of contacting Dad, though."

"No."

I glanced up at the letter that Dad had given me for Mum on the mantelpiece over the fireplace. I wondered what was in it and if we'd ever see Dad again. I know he'd said he was only going for a few weeks, but I had this feeling that he might be gone longer. I was sad. It had felt weird standing in my parents' room last night, looking at all that emptiness and wondering where they were.

Briony appeared. She yawned, and pulled the big chair up to the table. She was wearing a baggy black T-shirt that came down to her knees and a chunky wooden necklace from which dangled a silver bat.

"I like the bat," I said.

She held it in her palm, as if noticing it for the first time. "Oxfam shop." She yawned again. "What time is it?"

"Three," Jaz said. "You should be ashamed of yourself, getting up so late." She plonked a huge plate of baked beans in front of Briony. Several beans fell on to the table. Jaz liked cooking so, with a little persuasion from Elizabeth, she'd agreed to be chef while Mum and Dad were away.

"Beans?" Briony wiped her glasses on her T-shirt and put them on. She peered theatrically at the plate. "An unusual breakfast choice. Have the Munchy Malcolms all gone?"

"It's lunch," Elizabeth said.

Jaz brought in the rest of the plates and a pile of toast, and we tucked in.

"What's this?" Sammi picked up the greenery Jaz had arranged on top of the beans.

"Parsley," Jaz said. "It gives the beans a touch of class. Elevates them from the mundane to the spectacular. And it's good for you."

"It's stinky." Sammi tossed the parsley across the kitchen. "Here, Kevin."

Killer bashed the parsley with his huge paw,

sniffed at it and devoured it in one gulp.

There was silence for a while as we all tucked into the food. I hadn't realised how hungry I was.

"So – you win the getting-up-late prize," Jaz told Briony.

"Well, I was late going to bed," Briony said.

"We all were," Elizabeth said. "I don't think Mum would have been best pleased. I think we should decide upon a proper time for bed and then stick to it."

"We haven't heard from Mum, then?" Briony asked.

"Kind of," I said. "She rang this morning."

"Good," Briony said. "When is she coming home?"

"She talked to Sammi," Elizabeth said, "and Sammi forgot to mention the fact that Dad had gone as well."

"Sorry," Sammi said.

"So she's not coming home? And she's not going to send us any money?"

Elizabeth shook her head.

"I've been thinking," Briony said. "We can order food on the internet, but we could do with some cash as well."

"I've got. . ." Sammi started to say.

"Seven pounds twenty-three?" I said.

"And some Euros. . ." Sammi finished.

"That's great, Sammi," Briony said. "And my idea is that we all pool what cash we have. I've got nearly thirty pounds."

"That makes sense," I said. "I've got a ten pound note. And some change. There's probably some in my room. And I'll check my pockets."

"And we could look down the back of the sofa," Sammi said.

"I've got some," Elizabeth said. "Probably twenty quid. How about you, Jaz?"

"No way!" Jaz said. "It's a silly idea, anyway. Couldn't we get some from the cash machine? Briony knows Mum's PIN."

"It's not that easy," Briony said. "You need the actual card. Anyway – I make it seventy pounds that we can raise."

"And we could cash my Euros," Sammi said.

"We could look in Dad's jackets and coats, too," I suggested.

"Come on, Jaz," Briony said. "How much have you got?"

"But it's not fair. . . I've been saving up for a new pair of shoes and a top and that dress I told you about. . ."

"How much?"

"About sixty pounds. But I want it back!"

"That's settled, then," Briony said. "One hundred and thirty pounds. That should keep us going, if we're careful."

"I've just remembered," said Elizabeth. "We had a card from Dad. Look."

Briony put her knife and fork down and examined the card. "The White Cliffs of Dover. Money to pay. I wonder who the rock star is."

"Someone dead exciting, I expect," Jaz said. "Like Amber Lite."

"Or Robert Smith," Briony said.

"He's ancient," Jaz said.

"It's nothing to do with age," Briony replied. "Anyway, he lives in a mansion somewhere."

"But he's so gloomy."

"At least The Cure are a proper band. Amber Lite . . . she's just lightweight pop."

"She's not, she's. . ."

"That's enough!" I yelled.

"We had a visitor," Elizabeth said, and told Briony all about Mrs Herring. "She's Polish. She's retired now, but she used to be an estate agent."

"She didn't sell Mum and Dad this place,

did she?" Briony asked.

"No, she didn't."

"Good. I don't think I'd want to meet the person responsible for that. I might say something I'd regret."

"What are were going to do this evening, then?" I asked.

"Anyone fancy another game of Dracula?" Briony suggested.

"No fangs," Jaz said. "Geddit?"

"Very funny," I said.

"I know a fun thing you can do, Wilf," Jaz said.

"What's that?"

"The washing up."

I washed and Elizabeth dried.

"We should try and get the dishwasher fixed," I said.

"There's nothing wrong with it," Elizabeth said. "It's just that Mum said we mustn't use it because of the dodgy wiring in the house."

"I've had an idea," I said.

"To rewire the house?"

"No. Something else. We've been here a fortnight and the place doesn't look any different from when we arrived, does it? It still looks like the Little House of Horrors."

"Yes, but it takes time to sort things out. Mum's cleaned most of the rooms – more or less."

"I know. But what if we cleaned the café up? That would be good, wouldn't it?"

"I'm not sure," Elizabeth said.

"We could get it scrubbed up and shipshape. Although I do quite like it the way it is. You know – café-shaped."

"Very funny."

"But what do you think?" I asked her.

"I think you're crazy."

"But it just needs some elbow grease and a spot of paint."

"It would take an army to clean it. It'll take years. All that soot on the walls . . . how do you get that off?"

"It won't take years," I said. "We were going to do it anyway. We'll do it as a surprise for Mum and Dad. For when they get back."

"It sounds like hard work to me."

"We could decorate it, too."

"You're mad."

"What else can we do? Sit on the beach in the rain every day?"

I handed Elizabeth the last plate and dried my hands. "Let's see what the others say."

I went through into the PGR. Elizabeth put the last plate away and followed me.

"Listen up, everyone," I said. "I've had an idea."

Briony was reading a book – something to do with computer code. Jaz was playing with Sammi. It looked as if they were making clothes from silver foil for Sammi's teddy bears.

"I hope it's nothing like your last one," Jaz said.

"You mean organising a sports day at the old people's home?" I said. "That was a brilliant idea. We raised nearly a hundred pounds for Comic Relief."

"Sure," Jaz said. "And three people had to go to hospital."

"That wasn't my fault. The old people loved it. It was a huge success."

"Except for the three-legged race," Jaz said. "It was more like ten pin bowling. With human pins."

"And the wheelbarrow race was peculiar," Elizabeth added.

"That went well," I said. "It was a great idea to

use real wheelbarrows. Anyway, this isn't about a sports day. I think we should do up the café."

"That's not much of an idea. We've always been going to do that," Briony said.

"No, I mean now. Let's do it up for Mum and Dad. Before they get back. We'll clean it and decorate it. We could do a fantastic job on it. What do you think?"

"Yeah, all right," Jaz said.

"OK," Sammi said.

"Why not?" Briony said.

I looked at them, astounded. I never thought they'd agree. "Well, let's do it, then," I said.

"I'm not sure," Elizabeth said. "It will be so much work. And it's a lot of responsibility. What if something goes wrong?"

"Come on," Briony said. "It will give us something to do."

"I guess. . ." Elizabeth said.

"That's settled, then," Jaz said. "Now. . . let's get serious. An afternoon of Dracula, anyone?"

There was a choking sound.

"Kevin!" Sammi yelled. Killer was retching. She stroked his back and made soothing noises. "There, there, you lickle precious pussy cat. Get it all up. That's it."

The cat continued to retch violently, finally projecting a big dollop of green, frothy spit on the floor.

"I don't think parsley agrees with him," I said.

8
Russian Icons

Instead of playing cards, I decided to search out the art gallery. I'd been meaning to do it since we arrived, and talking to Mrs Herring about Rubens had reminded me.

The gallery was much bigger than I'd expected. It was in part of the town hall, a huge Victorian building. It took ages to find, even though I asked lots of people where it was. Four times I was told, "Sorry, I'm not from round here." And so it was getting late by the time I walked up the great curving stone steps and through the huge wooden doors covered in carvings and brass doo-dahs. I've never been a great fan of brass doo-dahs – I've always preferred brass whatsits, but the doo-dahs did add to the impressiveness of the doors. The sign said that the gallery closed at six – but an hour would be plenty of time for a quick look round. If there was anything I liked, I could always come back for another look. The great thing about looking at paintings is that you get ideas for your own work.

I wandered through the massive rooms, my footsteps echoing behind me. The gallery was deserted – just me, the faint smell of polish and the ghosts of our painterly past. Most of the rooms were full of pictures from Victorian times and earlier. They were big and gloomy, looming over me from their ornate frames hung high on the gallery walls. Some of the pictures were all right. Some, I thought, were pretty second rate. I couldn't see a Rubens anywhere.

The most interesting room featured early 20th-century paintings. There were a couple of Picassos and some Impressionists. Not bad for a small town like this. There were quite a few Russian paintings by artists I didn't recognise: Evstafiev, Kustodiev, Malevich. It looked as if the gallery had acquired a job lot. The Malevich was a red square on a plain white background. I figured it must have taken him all of half an hour to paint. I liked it, mind you.

The most interesting find was a Kandinsky, one of my favourite artists. The painting was called *Murnau Express* and showed an old-fashioned steam train painted a dark brown, chugging past brightly painted houses and trees, all in vivid greens and reds and golds. A smudge of steam hung over the scene. I was admiring it, when a voice startled me.

"Don't like the modern stuff myself." It was one of the attendants, a small man with a curly white moustache. "No, much too easy."

"What?"

"It's easy, painting like that. A two year old could do that."

"Do you think so?" I said. It seemed an odd thing for someone working in an art gallery to say. "It looks easy," I went on, "but I think there's actually a lot of technique involved."

The man sniffed and pulled out a large, grubby hanky. "Technique? Hah! Don't make me laugh. Artists today wouldn't know what technique was if it came and tipped a bucket of white emulsion over their heads. Modern rubbish. And look at that one. It's just a red square. Where's the skill, eh?"

"I like contemporary painting," I said. "What about that Kandinsky? That's skilfully done."

"Not really," he said. "Seen one, you've seen 'em all." He blew his nose. The noise echoed round the walls. "We've got a Jackson Pollock. Supposed to be worth a fortune. Looks like someone's laid the canvas on the floor and dribbled paint all over it. Bloomin' mess."

I didn't like to explain that that's exactly how

Pollock did paint his masterpieces.

"You an artist, then?" he asked. "That how you know about technique? Do the modern stuff yourself, do you?"

"Well, I do paint, yes." I didn't think this guy was going to be keen on comics, so I didn't mention my drawings. "I suppose you're a fan of the Old Masters, are you?"

"Ah," he said, "now you're talking. They knew how to paint in those days. Do you want to see something a bit special?"

"OK...," I said. I wasn't sure that I did. Old Masters have never really appealed to me. "Do you have anything by Rubens?"

"A couple of sketches. But it's not those I want to show you. Come with me." The attendant shoved the hanky back into his pocket and wiped his nose with the back of his hand. Then he turned and walked away. "Hurry up!"

Well, I was curious, so I followed him. He led the way at a brisk pace through several more rooms hung with impossibly huge paintings in dull brown oils, down a narrow marble staircase with a shiny brass banister covered in more brass doo-dahs, and along a gloomy corridor hung with gloomy portraits of gloomy kings and queens.

"It's a bit gloomy," I said.

"Have to keep them down here. It's the light, for one thing. It affects the paint. And the alarm system, of course. They're valuable things. Treasures!"

"The Kandinsky must be valuable, and that's upstairs," I said.

"Do you know what the gallery paid for that?"

"No."

"Too much. Hah!"

We were now standing in a small room with six small wooden paintings in a line along one wall. Each was protected by a sheet of glass and surrounded by small twinkling lights which would no doubt set off alarms if you got too close.

"Small, aren't they?"

They were. They all showed biblical scenes painted in bright colours, with lots of gold that glinted in the dim spotlights. Adam and Eve sat beneath a tree – a serpent coiled round its trunk. Another showed the Virgin Mary and the baby Jesus.

"Now, that's what I call technique," the attendant said. "Gorgeous – or what?"

"Yes," I said. "There *is* something about them." The little paintings weren't actually my thing. But they

55

were fascinating – exquisite, even.

"Russian icons," he said. "Painted on wood. Seven hundred years old. And guess what?"

"What?"

"They were stolen once."

"Really?"

"Really. See that one – that's my favourite. Painted by Rublev. He was made a saint."

The painting showed three figures, all with golden halos, gathered round a chalice on a low table. They were dressed in bright yellow, blue and green robes.

"We got them back. The thief was caught," he went on. "He's in prison now. But someone else might try again. That's why we have the hi-tech alarms. They're small, these icons. Easy to pop under your coat, eh? When Russia was part of the Soviet Union, nobody there wanted them. The Communists didn't approve of them because they're religious, see, so the people in charge, the KGB or whatever, confiscated them and either destroyed them or sold them. And there were plenty of buyers in Europe and America. But now that the Soviet Union is no more, the Russians want them back. They'll pay good money for them, too. Understandable. They're part of Russia's heritage."

We stared at them, me and the attendant, in that dark silence.

"Yes," the attendant said quietly. "I often come down here and spend time with them." He glanced at his watch. "Nearly six. Hurry up! Time to close."

I made my way back up to the main floor where I paid a quick visit to the shop, had a look at the postcards and books – nothing on comic art, I noted – and headed for home.

I wondered what was for supper. Baked beans, I wouldn't be surprised.

9
The Ghost Returns

I woke up and glanced at the clock. Two o'clock in the morning. Outside, the wind was howling like a demented rock singer and the rain was playing drums on the roof. In the distance I could hear the sea, like a class of infants playing violins in assembly. It was strange, lying in a different room from the one I'd grown up in. I didn't see this room as mine yet. It felt odd.

I was thinking about our plan to do up the café. If we managed to do that, then the next logical step would be to actually *open* the café. It couldn't be that hard, could it? I thought I might paint comic characters on the walls, Superman and the Silver Surfer. Then we could link the food we served to the paintings. We could have a comics theme throughout: Spiderman Soup followed by Batman Burgers and Captain Fury Fries. Or Dracula Doughnuts. Doughnuts you could sink your teeth into. Briony would like that. With jam that squirted out like blood. Yeah, maybe go with more of a horror theme.

I was getting quite involved in my plans when I heard that noise again. The ghost? Fear tied itself into a little knot in my stomach. Maybe it was just the wind. Then, above the noise of the wind and the rain, there was a terrible scream. It was Sammi!

If something had happened to Sammi, what would we do? What would Mum say? Maybe Killer had finally attacked her, bitten off her arm. I tried not to think about this as I scrambled down the stairs two at a time. Briony, Elizabeth and Jaz were close on my heels.

Sammi's face, white as chalk, was peering over the top of her duvet. Jaz pushed past me and put her arm around her sister and hugged her. Sammi began sobbing softly.

"It was the ghost," she whispered. "It was here."

Elizabeth sat on Sammi's other side and put her arm around her, too.

"It's OK," Elizabeth said. "It's not here now. It's gone."

"I heard it," Sammi said. "And I felt it touch me. That's when I. . . when I. . ."

"It's OK, babe," Elizabeth said, just like Mum did. "It's all right. The ghosty's gone."

"Don't leave me," Sammi said.

"I'll sleep with you tonight," Jaz said. "The ghost won't dare come if I'm here."

"Can Kevin sleep here?"

"Of course he can. Tomorrow night you can have Kevin to guard you."

Mum and Dad had a strict rule about pets in the bedrooms. But I thought they probably wouldn't mind if they knew about the ghost.

"You were probably dreaming," Briony said to Sammi. "Ghosts don't really exist. They're figments of our imagination."

"Figments? Do figments make scary noises?" Sammi asked.

"Let's all get back to bed," Elizabeth said. "We need our sleep. Night, night."

"What do you make of that, then?" I whispered, as we climbed the stairs back to our rooms.

"There's bound to be a rational explanation," Briony said.

"But Sammi's right. There *is* a ghost. I heard it last night. This house is haunted," Elizabeth said.

"That's rubbish," Briony said. We were standing on the little landing outside our rooms.

"But if it is haunted," I said, "that could be a selling point."

"What do you mean?" Elizabeth asked.

"When Mum and Dad open the café. I could paint scary pictures on the walls. We could hang strands of cotton up, so it feels like cobwebs – like we did at Hallowe'en. That was scary."

"Only because you're scared of spiders," Elizabeth said.

"No I'm not!"

Elizabeth laughed. "You are! You're scared of spiders!"

"But it's not haunted," Briony insisted.

"Ah," I said. "But Mrs Herring said there'd been a murder in the cellar hundreds of years ago. And just before Sammi screamed, I heard the ghost. Just like last night. A voice. And it was kind of moaning."

"Well I didn't hear anything," Briony said. "It was the wind. It's blowing a gale out there."

Back in my room, I lay in the darkness listening to the wind and the crashing swell of the sea. Briony was right, of course. There's no such thing as ghosts. But I thought about last night and about the noise I'd heard just before Sammi screamed. And I thought about what Mrs Herring had said about the murder in the cellar. And I turned my bedside light back on.

Just in case.

10
Here Comes
the Sun

I could hear the wind whistling through the attic rooms and the lofts somewhere over my head. I could hear the scritch, scratch of Vampyre's claws on the ancient roof slates. I knew it was trying to find a way in and soon it would succeed. Once in, it would soon find the door to my room. And I could do nothing. I could only offer it the key in return for my life. But what would my life be worth to such a creature? It would kill me and take the key anyway. Then make its way down to the cellar to release its master, the Gargoyle.

There was a crash somewhere above me. A gust of wind blew my window shutters wide open and the light of the full moon fell on to my face...

"Up you get, brother dearest," Elizabeth said.

I opened my eyes. The sun was streaming through the window.

"Day One of the Big Clean-up," Elizabeth said. "And I think that summer's finally arrived."

I made a garumphing noise and hid under the duvet.

"No point making a garumphing noise and hiding under the duvet," Elizabeth said. "The sun is out and the Big Clean-up beckons."

"I'm not getting up until everyone else is up."

Elizabeth yanked the duvet off me and deposited it on the floor. I jumped up and grabbed my boxers.

"Everyone is up. Even Briony. And breakfast is ready. Guess what we're having?" But, before I could say, "Sausage, eggs, bacon, tomatoes, fried bread and mushrooms," in a hopeful tone, she'd gone.

I stood in the patch of sunlight, feeling the sun on my bare skin, and stretched. Lovely. We should be on the beach, not cleaning the café. But I couldn't complain. After all, it was my idea. I peered out of the window. Down in the yard, Sammi was laying a trail of breadcrumbs. It looked as if she was trying to catch Gerald, the rat.

Sunshine. Maybe the sunshine was a good omen that everything was going to be all right. I pulled my clothes on. No point in washing. I'd only be getting dirty again.

And breakfast? Well, it was beans, of course. Jaz was becoming a bit of an expert. For two days we'd had beans served in interesting and various ways: on toast, like now, but also bean soup, bean pie . . .

and bean surprise. Bean surprise for supper last night had looked like a shepherd's pie. A lovely, gleaming, steaming potato crust and underneath, the surprise – no shepherd, just baked beans. I have to say, though, I was getting a bit fed up with them. And so was my bottom.

So it was a relief when the Tesco order arrived after breakfast. We stood in the kitchen gazing at the array of carrier bags.

"You're so clever, Briony," Elizabeth said. "I could never have sorted out how to order all that food over the internet – sort out the payment and everything."

"It was easy," Briony said. "All you have to do is tick what you want and then choose a date and time for it to be delivered. Well – and put in your credit card details. But then, I helped Mum save those on the computer the other day, so that was no problem, because I know the security code."

"There seem to be rather a lot of cakes and doughnuts," Jaz said.

"Really?" Briony gave us an innocent look.

"All that temptation," Elizabeth said. "That's not fair on me."

"Don't eat them, then," Jaz said.

"It's not my fault that I put on weight so easily. I just

have a slower metabolism, that's all," Elizabeth said.

I grabbed a carrier bag and tried to lift it. It was heavy. "It's a pity about the rice."

Briony sighed. "Yeah, I didn't mean to order that much. I just wasn't sure how much eight kilograms of rice was. It was a bargain buy."

"You'll get it right next time," Elizabeth said.

We all stared at the rice. There were carrier bags full. If we ate rice every day for a year, there would still be some left over.

"I wonder if Gerald likes rice," Sammi said.

We started the Big Clean-up in the kitchen. It would have been easier working in a coal mine, digging out the coal with your fingers. Someone had had a go at getting rid of the fire damage, but still, everything was covered with a thick layer of black grease. Briony had got my digital camera working – something to do with the batteries and the card – and she took lots of photos. She said she was recording the transformation. We'd bought lots of cleaning stuff from Tesco's which the adverts said would lift the most stubborn dirt and grease from every surface. Not true. Adverts lie.

It took all day to get the kitchen equipment clean. And another thing about cleaning products that they don't tell you in the adverts – they make the skin on your hands and fingers shrivel up.

Well, we finished around four, absolutely done in. So as a special treat we took ourselves down to the beach for a swim.

In the evening, the sky clouded over and thunder rumbled in the distance. It was nine o'clock and getting dark – very dark, on account of the black clouds building up overhead. Elizabeth and I were sitting in the gloomy café ruminating upon how we might proceed. I like *ruminating*. It's a great word. It reminds me of cows wandering around in a field wondering which area of grass they might tackle next. *Ruminating* is one of Dad's words. He's brilliant with words. I do miss him.

There was a loud rumble and something fell from the ceiling, making me jump.

"Was that a spider?"

"No," Elizabeth said. "Just bits of plaster and cobwebs."

"Not that I'd mind if it *was* a spider," I said. "I was just curious." I brushed the bits off the table. "I've been thinking. Instead of just cleaning and decorating the café, why don't we go the whole hog – and open it?"

Elizabeth stared at me, sighed, and slowly shook her head.

I pushed the little red plastic umbrella aside with my finger and took a long swallow on my Coke and ice. "It would be brilliant," I insisted. "And great fun. We could have a big opening ceremony."

Elizabeth took a sip of her lime and soda, nudging her little pink umbrella aside with her nose. "But it would just mean more work. What's the point?"

I'd given this some thought. "Mum and Dad always tell us that they love one another really, even though they argue all the time. Right?"

Elizabeth nodded.

"And what do they argue about?"

"Dad's hopelessness?"

"He isn't hopeless," I said. "He just lives in a slightly different way from everyone else. Part of his brain is actually in a different dimension, and this causes him to act in unusual and unexpected ways. He's a very creative person."

"Yeah, hopeless. That's what I said. I do love him, but he *is* hopeless."

More thunder rumbled overhead. It was now darker than ever and hot and muggy. I rubbed the icy-cold glass against my forehead. "The answer I was looking for," I said, "is money. They argue about money. That's why buying this place was important to them. A joint project that would raise a good income."

"But it won't," Elizabeth said. "It's rubbish."

"It has huge potential. I'm going to paint comic book heroes all over the walls. And we'll serve brilliant food, like Batman Burgers. And have a juke box with really cool music. And live bands. There's nothing like that in this town. It's a dump. And Mum and Dad will come home and the café will be all finished and making money. And then our lives can get back to normal."

"I'm not convinced."

"Let's have a meeting and ask the others. If they say no, I'll forget all about it."

"OK."

"Brilliant! That's what we'll do, then."

There was a blinding flash and an almighty explosion that rocked the café and made me jump out of my seat. The old wooden furniture rattled. More bits fell from the old beams above. I looked up anxiously for falling spiders.

"That was close," Elizabeth said.

"Don't worry," I said. "This building's been here hundreds of years. A thunderstorm's not going to hurt it. I bet it's survived thousands of thunderstorms."

Outside, the trap door in the big black cloud fell open and it began to rain. Torrential rain.

Sammi appeared with Killer wrapped in her arms. "Kevin's scared," she said. "His fur is standing on end."

"Killer is scared? Did I hear you right?" I asked.

Then the lights went out and somebody screamed.

11
Thumbs

We sat in the pitch blackness. The rain was trying its hardest to break the windows. And the wind was giving it a hand.

"Who was that screaming?" I asked.

"Jaz, I think," Elizabeth said.

"It's OK. . . There, there. . ." I could hear Sammi calming the cat.

"Hello?" I could hear the forlorn voice of Jaz from somewhere in the house and the movement of chairs as she stumbled towards us in the darkness. There was a clump and a clatter as some furniture fell over.

"This way," Elizabeth called.

"I don't suppose there's a torch anywhere," I said. "Or candles?"

"What's that?" Sammi cried, and pointed to the window.

There was a circle of light outside the grimy, rain-soaked pane – and it was getting closer. A dark figure appeared outside the door. The beam of light cast long shadows around the room.

The figure banged on the door.

"It's the ghost," Sammi whispered.

"Don't be silly," Jaz said.

"I'm scared," Sammi said. "I think it's a figment."

We stared at the dark shape, hunched over like a grotesque monster. The figure banged on the door again.

"Let me in." Its voice was faint, almost lost in the pouring rain. "I'm getting bleedin' soaked."

Jaz felt her way past the old furniture and opened the door. Rain gusted in and the figure entered. Jaz shut the door behind him as he took the mac off his head, shook it and hung it on the back of a chair.

"What a night," he said. "I'm Ivan."

"Hello, Ivan," Elizabeth said.

"But everybody calls me Thumbs."

He put his torch on the table. It was a big square one and it lit the room with a pale yellow light. "When the lights went out, I thought to myself that you just might need a hand. I own the shop over the road."

I guessed he meant the one selling security equipment and locks. I'd looked in the window once or twice. It was dusty and neglected. It didn't look like a thriving business. Thumbs was small and lumpy with a leathery face and piercing eyes that reflected the yellow torchlight. I looked at his hands. His thumbs looked pretty average.

"Where's your mum, then?" he asked. "I haven't seen her coming or going. No, I haven't."

"Um . . . she's been at a friend's today and this evening," I said.

"Don't worry about the power cut," he said. "We get them all the time here. There you are. The power's back. The cuts don't last long."

"But it's still dark," Jaz said.

"Look out there."

Sure enough, there was a light in his shop and you could see the faint glow of the street light.

"Yeah," he said. "It's your wiring. It's kaput. I was always telling John he should have it seen to. Yeah, have it seen to. It's lucky you've got any lights at all, I reckon. As soon as the power went, I thought to myself, best get over the road, give those people a hand. How about your dad, then? Where's he?"

"Working abroad," Elizabeth said.

"There you are, then. Lucky I was at home. I'm an electrician, see. Qualified. I could sort it out for you. No trouble."

"Good," Elizabeth said.

"Why are you called Thumbs?" Sammi asked.

The man chuckled. "Because I'm good with locks, of course. I wanted everyone to call me Fingers – but they said that was too obvious and it made me sound like a criminal, so we settled for Thumbs instead."

"Well, you wouldn't want to sound like a criminal," Elizabeth said.

"Come on," Thumbs said, "let's find the fuse box."

He stood up, catching the edge of the table with his hip. The torch toppled on to the floor and went out. He swore.

We waited patiently while he retrieved the torch and got it working again.

"Sorry about that," he said. "Fuse box. C'mon!" We followed him into the kitchen. "Bet you've explored this place pretty well."

"I guess so," I said.

"Found any hidden treasure? Anything unusual?"

"Well," Sammi said, "there's Gerald."

"Gerald?"

"The rat."

The lights came on and there was Briony standing by the fuse box in the kitchen. "I just changed the fuse," she said. "I saw all the other lights in the road were on and put two and two together. It's a pretty decrepit fuse box."

"You're not wrong there," Thumbs said. "So, who are you?"

Elizabeth introduced us all. "Would you like a cup of tea?" she asked him.

He shook his head. "Nah, best be off. Best be off."

We followed him to the door and he put the mac back over his head. "If you need anything, give us a call. Always happy to help. I like to feel useful, you know. I could do the wiring."

"Would you?" I asked.

"Yeah, of course. I'm pretty cheap. Have a word with your folks."

"We will," Elizabeth said. "And thank you."

"You're welcome. You're welcome." He struggled with the door for a bit, trying to turn the latch, and then shaking and rattling it.

"It's a bit stiff," I said, tactfully. "There's a knack to it."

I opened the door and let him out. And we watched him shuffle across the road in the rain, drop the torch again, and finally let himself into his run-down shop.

12
Let's Put the Show on Right Here

The next day, the weather returned to normal. Summer was back and had brought with it a dull, colourless sky and some misty rain.

On the bright side, there was a card from Mum. The donkey on the front wasn't very well drawn. I could have done better. It was wearing a straw hat. It was wishing we were there. Well, that's probably what it was wishing, but the speech bubble was in Spanish. Maybe it was saying "Good morning, suckers."

Mum was having a lovely break in Spain. She hoped we were well. She hoped Dad was managing. There was no address and the postmark was blurry. She said she was missing us terribly and was planning to come home before the August Bank Holiday, probably on the Saturday. We looked at the calendar. Just over two weeks away.

We were sitting round the big oak table in the morning gloom. We'd eaten our breakfasts and were looking forward to some more work in the kitchen.

Not. This seemed a good opportunity to tell everyone about my new plan.

"I've had an idea," I told my sisters.

Briony groaned. "Does it involve more work?"

"Is it: let's stop all this cleaning nonsense and go to the pictures?" Jaz asked. "*Mary Poppins* is on at the Odeon."

"You're joking," Elizabeth said. "That film's a billion years old. And everyone will have seen it on DVD."

"No – Mary Poppins is cool again."

"She came to see us," Sammi said. "She's going to teach us to fly."

"No, that wasn't Mary Poppins," I said. "It was someone who wanted to be our cleaner."

"That's right, Mary Poppins *is* a cleaner," Sammi said. "But she has magic."

"I know," I said. I was beginning to get a little cross. "My idea. . ."

"You're not going to suggest we buy a magic wand, are you?" Jaz asked.

"No. My idea. . ."

"Because we couldn't afford it," Jaz went on.

"My idea. . ."

"You can't buy magic wands," Sammi said.

"I won't tell you, then," I said.

"Do tell us your idea, brother dearest," Jaz said.

"No."

"Go on," Elizabeth said. "Take no notice of Jaz."

"You can buy them in Diagon Alley," Sammi added. "It is a difficult place to find, mind, if you're not a wizard."

"My idea. . ." And I waited for another interruption, but there wasn't one this time, ". . . is not only to clean and decorate the café, but to reopen it."

"What?" Jaz said. "How can we do that?"

I outlined my plan. And I explained how we could do it as a surprise for Mum and have a grand Bank Holiday opening when she got home.

After a lot of discussion, we voted.

"I'm against," Elizabeth said. "It will take until then just to clean it. And we know nothing about running a café. It will all end in disaster."

"I like the idea," Jaz said. "I'll be the chef. Like those chefs on the telly. I'll get myself one of those tall white hats."

"I agree too," Sammi said.

"I'm in," Briony said, "but I don't know what I'll be able to do."

"There's loads of stuff," I said. "Advertising. Lots of organisation. You're good at that. Ordering food.

Printing menus. All stuff you can do on the computer. And you can be the waitress, Elizabeth. What do you think?"

"What do I think? I think that everyone else gets fun jobs and I have to be the boring old waitress."

"Yes," I said, "because you're so good with people."

Elizabeth sighed. "I suppose I'll agree, then, if everybody else wants to do it. But I still think it's a stupid idea. OK – I'm in."

Everybody cheered.

"So, if we've only got two weeks," Elizabeth added, "we'd better get a move on with the cleaning. Come on. Back to work."

Everybody groaned.

"Can we go and see *Mary Poppins* afterwards?" Sammi asked.

Late afternoon, and the kitchen was more or less done. The scariest bit was cleaning underneath the cookers and getting into all the nooks and crannies. The largest spider I've ever seen ran out, and I dropped an oven tray. A great glob of fatty stuff splattered all over my trainers and jeans. I wasn't scared of it – the spider, I mean, not the globby fat. It startled me, that was all. The spider was the size of a golf ball. Sammi caught it in a jar and let it go in the shed. She said it would be a friend for Gerald.

Now I was sitting in my room, working out some designs for the café walls. After rejecting several names for the café (Jaz suggested The Pink Doughnut, as she said that was her favourite colour and her favourite food) we decided on The Comic Café. And, as the artist in the family, I now had the task of decorating the walls.

I'd considered some of my favourite comic characters like Vampyre and the Gargoyle, but I thought vampires and zombies might actually put the paying public off. So I'd decided it would be best to go for more popular characters like Superman, Batman and the Silver Surfer. I'd also thought about copying some Roy Lichtenstein paintings onto the walls. Making it really classy. I don't know if you've seen his paintings, but they're all scenes from comics and the pictures have titles like *Wham!* He blows them up really huge and paints them in big bold colours. I wondered if there were any of his paintings in the art gallery.

So, I was making some rough sketches when a

shadow passed over the paper. I glanced up as the huge white monster passed in front of the window. A really scary monster – scary to seagulls, that is. It was Killer, climbing across my windowsill.

I watched him climb up on to the roof where there was a ledge, and settle down to wait. On the chimney pot sat a massive seagull. Killer was staring at the seagull. The seagull was staring at Killer. Seagulls can be dangerous if they attack you. They're very strong, with powerful beaks. But I felt sorry for this one. I didn't fancy its chances against our cat.

13
Would You Buy a Used Car from This Man?

"Hard at vork?" Mrs Herring breezed into the café next morning as if she owned the place. She shook the wet from her giant black umbrella and stood it near the open door.

"Another day, another dollar," I said. It was something I'd heard in an American gangster movie once. Maybe it should be, "Another day, another pound". Or, "Another day, another Euro". That doesn't sound right, though, does it?

I was moving all the tables and chairs to one end of the room out of the way, ready to start cleaning the main eating area. We were going to have to throw most of the furniture away – it was old, dirty and broken. Briony was upstairs on the laptop, starting work on The Comic Café website, which was her idea. Perhaps she'd be able to find some cheap tables and chairs on eBay. Elizabeth and Jaz were sorting cutlery and cleaning pots and pans. I don't know where Sammi was. Probably still trying to catch ratty Gerald.

"Is your mozer in?" Mrs Herring asked.

"Um . . . no," I said. "She's . . . um . . . shopping at the moment. I . . . er . . . we . . . told her you called."

"Good. Are you looking for cleaner, then?"

"Well . . . um . . . we might be. Mum wasn't sure."

Mrs Herring gazed around the room. "Could I lend you hand, maybe? I'm at bit of loose end today."

Her offer took me by surprise. Why would she want to help? We'd only met her once. We didn't know anything about her. And did she mean she'd do it for free?

She noted my lack of enthusiasm.

"Vell, if you don't vant help. . ." she said, sounding a bit upset. "I'd have thought you'd be pleased to have anozer pair of hands."

"Well. . ."

"Zink of it as free try-out. And I can meet your mum when she gets home."

Well, what could I say? Of course she'd have to wait a long time before Mum came home. "OK, then. Of course we'd like you to help. The more, the merrier."

"Jolly good. I'll just go and change." She picked up her umbrella and glanced up at the grey sky. "Looks like it's going to clear up later."

As I lugged tables across the floor and piled up chairs in the corner, I wondered if I'd done the right thing. But we would need a cleaner – so why not Mrs Herring? I wondered what Elizabeth would say when she found out. Oh well. It'd be quite useful to have an extra pair of hands. I don't know where you'd put them, though – you'd have to have extra pockets.

"Excuse me, mate."

My reverie was interrupted by a gruff voice.

"Sorry," I said. "I was miles away."

A man in a smart, dark blue suit stood in the doorway. "Where were you, then? Somewhere sunny, I hope. Can I come in?"

"We're not open." I was stating the obvious, I know, but sometimes the obvious just hangs around waiting to be stated. Like Killer when he's in a bad mood, looking for a chance to bite your ankles.

"So that would be why there are no tablecloths," the man said. He walked up to me and shook my hand. "I'm Frank. Pleased to meet you."

"Hello," I said. "I'm Wilf."

The man handed me a business card from his top pocket.

Frank Meek
Motors (Antique)

"We do all sorts of wheels, actually. If you're in the market for a nice car, let me know. But vintage cars – that's my speciality."

I felt in my pocket and pulled out a comic trading card. I gave it to Frank.

"What's this?" he asked.

"The Incredible Hulk," I said. "One of the all-time greats."

"I see." He looked confused.

"You can keep it. It's one of my swaps. But if you come across Max Microbe, let me know. That's a very rare card."

"Ah. . ."

"You sell old cars, then," I said. "To be honest, I'm a bit young to drive."

"You're not the owner of this establishment, then?" I shook my head.

"This takes me back," he said, gazing around the room. "Used to come here a lot. Did some good . . . er . . . well, let's say, business deals here. It used to be called The Smugglers' Rest, you know."

That was news to me. "I thought it was called Rubens' Rest."

"Only for a little while. Originally it was an inn.

Yeah, The Smugglers' Rest. Used to be a lot of that in these parts."

"What? Resting?"

"Devon and Cornwall are famous for smuggling, of course. But there was a lot round here, too. All sorts of stuff used to be smuggled in along this coast. Tobacco, gin . . . even tea. In the 18th century there was a 119 per cent tax on tea. And at one time you weren't allowed to bring in anything from France. So they used to park their luggers just over the horizon and row the contraband in under cover of darkness."

"You know a lot about it."

"I was thinking of going in for *Mastermind*. But I don't think I'd cope with the general knowledge round. Are you going to open the café again?"

I nodded. "That's the plan. August Bank Holiday."

"Not long, then. Looks like you'll have your work cut out. Your mum or dad home?"

"No," I said. "Dad's away working. Mum's shopping."

"Well, like I say, good luck with it. Rather you than me."

Enter Briony. She was holding a camera.

"Good morning, young lady," Frank said.

Briony nodded.

"Er . . . nice dress."

She was wearing a rather tatty, full-length black silk dress. I say full length, but actually the hem formed a sort of train behind her as she walked. It was too big for her

"It's from Cancer Research," she said.

"Ah, well, I must be going," Frank said.

"Time and tide wait for no man," I said.

"Or woman," said Briony.

"Or smuggler," I added.

"Tell your folks I called."

"Another day, another packet of tea," I said.

"What was that all about?" Briony asked, when he'd gone.

I shrugged. "Another old customer. He wanted to sell me a car."

"You're too young to drive."

"Did you know this place was an inn before it was a café? It was called The Smugglers' Rest."

"Really?" Briony said. "Maybe I should do a bit of research. Find out a bit about the history of the place.

We could put it on the website."

"That would be cool. And see if you can find out about the murder, too. How's the website going?"

"Not too bad. I've got the basic layout done. I'll need a few pictures. Have you done the designs for the walls yet?" I shook my head. "And we'll need a logo."

"OK," I said. "I'll get on with it tonight."

"I'm taking some more photos for the album." She was looking round the room. "The original walls have been boarded over, haven't they? They kept the old beams on the ceiling."

"Hello again!" Mrs Herring came in. She was wearing a black track suit and spotless white trainers. She certainly looked more like a cleaner now, although the track suit looked new. It wouldn't be in that condition for long, once she started on this place.

"Reporting for duty. Vere vould you like me to start?"

"You must be Mrs Poppins," Briony said.

Mrs Herring looked at her blankly.

"This is Mrs Herring," I told Briony. "She's going to help us clean the place up."

"Da . . . er, yes. I am."

"Mrs Herring, this is Briony."

"Zat is nice dress," Mrs Herring said. "I like colour. Black. It is my favourite. It is very long. And belt is beautiful."

"British Heart Foundation," Briony said.

There was a hiss. Killer was staring at our new cleaner in a scary, move-you're-blocking-my-path kind of way.

"Get zat monster away from me," Mrs Herring cried.

"Smile, please," Briony said. And took her picture.

14
Good Day Sunshine

"Getting pooed on by a seagull is supposed to be lucky? You're telling me that it's lucky having a big dollop of mucky, sticky, stinky, fishy white bird poo land on your head?"

I fished in my pocket for a tissue.

"So they say," Briony said. "I didn't make it up."

Jaz started singing "I Should Be So Lucky".

"It must be very lucky to have a cow poo on your head then," Sammi said.

"And what's very, very lucky," Briony said, "is having an elephant poo on your head."

"Amber Lite covered 'I Should Be So Lucky'," Jaz said.

"I'm not surprised," Briony replied. "You wouldn't catch The Cure doing a rubbish song like that."

We were walking along the seafront. Saturday. All five of us – like children from an Enid Blyton story. *The Famous Five Go Shopping For Chairs.* No cleaning today, as we'd decided to take the weekend off. It wasn't a bad seafront. And it wasn't raining. There were lots of clouds scudding about the sky, but every now and then the sun came out. Holidaymakers looked perplexed. What's that big, shiny, warm, yellow thing in the sky? People were actually smiling. Some were even laughing. Children were hopping and skipping along – that sort of thing.

Both Jaz and Briony had dressed up for the occasion. Jaz was wearing her white hoody T-shirt, puffy metallic blue jacket and silver boots. Briony was totally covered in black, including a black hat and black lipstick, something that Dad didn't approve of – well, he didn't mind lipstick in general, although he didn't wear it himself – he didn't like lipstick on Briony.

Two postcards had come from Dad this morning. The first one said he was seriously considering buying a motorbike. He'd got his heart set on a Harley Sportster. I couldn't really imagine him in a black leather jacket with a skull and crossbones on the back. He hoped we were all well. Love to Mum.

The second card was about meeting up for a game of darts when he got back. It started, "Dear Nigel", but was addressed to us. None of us knew who Nigel was. Nor had we heard of Purple Leopard, but Dad's card said that the famous rock musician he was working for used to be in a band called Purple Leopard. I thought I might search out one of their albums in a charity shop when I had time.

We spent the morning on the beach and ate the sandwiches we'd made for lunch. In the afternoon, Elizabeth stayed on the beach with Jaz and Sammi while Briony and I had a look around the old town. I was looking for chairs. Rather than buying an expensive set of new chairs for the café, I thought we'd buy some second-hand ones and paint them lots of bright, splashy colours. I hoped to find a Purple Leopard album, too, that Dad could get autographed for me. Briony, as always, was on the look-out for black second-hand clothes and old computer games.

We stopped for a while to watch a busker, a scruffy bloke wearing a faded and tatty silver-sequinned suit, playing a saxophone. He was pretty good. At the end of the song I threw a twenty-pence piece into his open sax case. I'm well known for my generosity.

"Bless yah, laddie," he said.

He looked old. That would be the prolonged effect of the outdoors, the wind and rain and the salt air, combined with the degenerating effect of all the excitement this town had to offer – late night bingo, donkey rides and high class cuisine. He was probably only a teenager.

"You on holiday?" he asked.

"Are you mad?" I said. "No, I live here."

"You don't sound like you come from round here," the man said, "and you have the pale look of a foreigner. You Scottish?"

I shook my head. "I went to Scotland once. But I came back."

"Just as well."

"Actually, we've not been here long. Our parents have bought an old café and we're helping them do it up."

The man grabbed my arm and peered into my face, as if he could see into my head, through my eyes. "Wouldn't be The Smuggler's Rest, would it?"

I nodded, and tried to smile. His grip on my arm tightened as I tried to pull away. Then he smiled a yellow smile.

"It'll be good to see that place open again," he said. "Thanks for the twenty pence. Very generous." He turned his attention to Briony. "Nice hat."

"Save the Children," she said.

"Ah," said the busker. He picked up his saxophone again. "Any requests?"

"Do you know anything by Purple Leopard?" I asked.

He winked. "Course I do. I'm very fond of the old heavy metal."

He pushed a footswitch and the backing track started. He put the sax to his lips and began to play "Good Day Sunshine". We listened for a bit, then continued on our way.

"Purple Leopard are better than I thought," Briony said.

"That was a Beatles number," I told her.

"He was a funny bloke. Bit scary."

"Mad busker. Every town's got one. You have to have one for the tourists. It's the law."

We met up late that evening. Everyone had had a great day. Jaz had met some girls by the arcades and made some new friends, including a boy she liked the look of called Didier – probably one of the French language students who seemed to favour this town, goodness knows why or how the council managed to persuade people to leave the sunny side of the Channel for this dump. But there seemed to be plenty of

French, Spanish and Italian students around.

Briony had found a stack of old computer games in a charity shop: *Aliens from the Planet Doom, Pongo Pongo, Monkey Up a Ladder. . .* She was excited, but they all looked pretty dire to me. I'd hit the jackpot with the chairs, though – a job lot of forty from a furniture warehouse. They were brand new, but what the warehouse manager called "seconds". That meant they all had some kind of minor defect. He showed me one and it had a bad scratch. That didn't matter, I explained to him, as we were going to paint them to match the room. And they were really, really cheap – eighty-five pounds the lot. He said he'd deliver them a week on Monday.

Elizabeth and Sammi were red and sore, even though Elizabeth had had the presence of mind to use sun cream. They'd eventually got bored with sitting on the beach and had done some shopping of their own. Goodness knows how Sammi had persuaded Elizabeth to buy a life-sized shop-window dummy. Sammi said it would make her feel better, having an adult in the house.

"But it's a dummy," I pointed out.

"That's good, then, isn't it?" Jaz said. "It won't be able to boss us about."

Of course, it had to be today that Mum phoned, while we were all out. Elizabeth played the answerphone message back. Mum said how much she was looking forward to seeing us all again. Told us how brilliant the weather was. And asked us to make sure Dad was working hard. She even said she was looking forward to seeing Dad, too.

As soon as the message stopped, Jaz, of all people, burst into tears. Elizabeth hugged her. A sobbing Jaz started Sammi crying. Seeing Jaz and Sammi crying was too much for Elizabeth, who joined in. As I fled the room, I noticed that Briony was dabbing at her eyes with a tissue.

In my room I stared out of the window at the overgrown yard. There was Gerald, nosing around. I felt tears pricking my eyes.

It was only because I felt sorry for the rat.

15
Hey Gerald, Where Are You Going with That Loaf in Your Mouth?

Sunday. A day of rest. The weather wasn't quite up to yesterday's standard. Overcast, but feeling quite warm. We went for a walk along the seafront. Jaz, in her Sunday best – fur-trimmed denim top and jeans and her silver boots – went off to find her new friends. She was wearing make-up. Watch out, Didier! I thought.

Sammi spent most of the afternoon trying to catch Gerald. She'd given up with the trails of breadcrumbs. The rice hadn't worked, either. Now she was using one of the sausages left over from last night's supper. In the shed she'd propped up a cardboard box on a stick, to which was tied a length of string. Under the box was the sausage. The idea was that Gerald would follow the scent of sausage into the shed and under the box. Sammi would then pull the string and the box would fall over Gerald, thus capturing him.

"We'll have to get the rat-catcher in," I told Sammi. "We can't have a rat around when we open the café. They'll close us down."

"I know," Sammi said. "That's why I'm going to catch him. I'm going to take him a long way away and let him go."

"He'll bite. Rats are full of diseases," Elizabeth said.

"Not true," Briony said. "They did a survey of over 500 cases of rats biting people, and not one person caught a disease from the bite. Rats are much maligned."

"Well, I wouldn't want a rat to bite me," Elizabeth said.

"Mind you, if we catch it, we could cook it," I suggested. "Make ratatouille." Everyone groaned. Sammi gave me a dirty look.

Of course, Elizabeth was right. Rats were dangerous. I'd have insisted Sammi got ride of the trap, but I knew there was no way it was going to work. For one thing, rats are very intelligent. No way was a rat going to fall for that old trick. And for another, the presence of Killer, sitting by the back door waiting patiently for Gerald to show, made the rat's appearance about as likely as Killer winning an Oscar for his sensitive performance in *The Fluffy Bunny Movie*.

Briony turned up some interesting information while she was doing research for our new website. Rubens' Rest had been owned by someone called John Montague. And John Montague had once been an art critic for *The Times*. Well, that made sense. I expect he'd done what our parents had done – retired to the seaside and opened a café. But he obviously hadn't made a go of it. As well as running the café, Briony told me, John Montague had worked at the art gallery.

"I've been there," I told her. "It's pretty good, considering the size of the town."

"They had a robbery," Briony said, "eight years ago. Six Russian icons were stolen, but they were recovered."

"I know about that," I said. "I bet the locals were beside themselves with excitement. I expect it's up there with the Moon landings and the time someone stubbed their toe on a pebble on the beach." Briony didn't laugh.

"I wonder why this John Montague person gave up on the café, though? And how long it was open for?" I went on. "It would be good not to make the same mistakes."

"I'll research it some more."

"Good idea. Find out where it went wrong – well, other than being stuck down a back alley in a second-rate seaside town with an allergy to sunlight, of course."

16
Bottoms

Nothing much happened on Monday and Tuesday other than cleaning, cleaning and more cleaning. We did some more cleaning, and then cleaned some more. The kitchen was looking very good by now, even if we were all sick to death of cleaning it.

On Wednesday, we moved rooms and started on the main eating area in earnest. Elizabeth, Jaz and myself had decided that it made sense to start from the ceiling and work down. I'd arranged the tables in groups of four, then put another table on top, in the middle. Thus, armed with buckets of hot soapy water and mops, we were going to attempt to clean the ceiling. And probably get very wet.

Which we did. We got soaked. It took all morning.

We were having lunch when Mrs Herring arrived. She was dressed smartly as usual and all in black. She and Briony had that in common. Maybe she had a part-time job at the undertaker's. She probably slept there at night, in a coffin. The absence of the track suit bottoms meant she hadn't come to lend a hand today, I guessed.

She asked after our health and wanted to see Mum. We gave her the usual excuse. I think she smelt a rat – and I don't mean Gerald.

"Have you mentioned me to your mozer? I'm sure she vould velcome someone to clean house. I vas good helper on Friday, vasn't I?"

"Yes," we all said together. It was true. She had been a great help cleaning the kitchen.

"We're going to open the café soon," said Sammi.

"Really?" Mrs Herring raised her eyebrows. "Not vaiting for Spring? Zat is vonderful."

"We've decided to open it for the August Bank Holiday," Elizabeth said.

"I can see vhy you're vorking so hard on it, zen." Mrs Herring allowed her eyebrows to gently lower themselves back into their normal position. "Let's see . . . zat is less zan two veeks avay. I'm sure your mozer vould velcome my help wiz cleaning."

"Oh yes," Elizabeth said. "We've told her about you. Mum says she's thinking about it."

"Zat's good," Mrs Herring said, "because I'm beginning to vonder if she exists."

There was an awkward silence that no one seemed to want to fill. Eventually Mrs Herring spoke again. "So . . . you're going to clean valls in here next?"

"That's right," I said. "We can't wait to see what the pictures are."

"I think they're elephants," Sammi said. "Did you know, it's very lucky to have an elephant poo on your head?"

There was another silence. This one was shorter but slightly more awkward.

"Of course it is," Mrs Herring said, "Da . . . yes . . . vell . . . must get on. . . I've got hair appointment. Say hello to your mum from me."

We all put on big smiles and bid her farewell.

"I wish she wouldn't keep going on about Mum," Elizabeth said. "She makes me nervous."

"You don't think she's from Social Services, do you?" Briony asked. "If they found out we were living here without a responsible adult, we could be in serious trouble."

"Don't be stupid. We live with Mum and Dad," Jaz said.

"But would you call them responsible adults?" I asked.

"Anyway," Jaz said, "it's not our fault they've both cleared off."

"What I mean," Briony said, "is that they could send us off to foster homes or something, you know, until

Mum or Dad get back. And I bet our parents could be prosecuted, too. For neglect."

"Do you think it's illegal, then?" Elizabeth said.

Briony shrugged. "Dunno. I'll have a look on the internet."

"Anyway, I'm going out this afternoon," Jaz said. "I'm meeting Kavita and Sandy at two."

"What about Didier?" I ventured.

"No. He turned out to be an OIF."

"Oif?"

"Only Interested in Football."

"Wouldn't that be an OI-IF?" I asked. "The letter *I* is repeated."

Jaz gave me a look.

"But what about the cleaning?" Elizabeth asked. "We're going to do the walls next. Don't you want to see what the pictures are?"

"I'll see when I get back, won't I? Anyway – I've done my share. This is supposed to be fun, isn't it? I'm going to change. I've got a new top. And Didier's best mate is interesting. He's called Joel. His family is from Trinidad. I'm thinking blazing sunshine, golden beaches, blue skies . . . a little reggae on the radio. . . See you later."

"I'm going as well," Sammi said. "I've got to

check my rat trap."

Jaz and Sammi left the room, leaving the three of us contemplating the task ahead.

"Let's have the remainder of the day off and carry on tomorrow," Briony suggested.

"We can't afford the time," I said. "There's still so much to do if we're going to open on schedule."

"You can have a rest," Elizabeth said to Briony, "but Wilf and I will do a bit more. And anyway, I'm curious about the pictures."

"OK, I'll give the cleaning a miss," Briony said. "But I'll do some more research."

It took the rest of the afternoon to get the walls clean. Briony had found out on the internet the best way to get soot off painted surfaces. We had to use special sponges and cleaner, which luckily we'd found in the hardware store up the road. It was hard work, but it was worth it – because what we found underneath the grime was astonishing.

Fat naked ladies!

"They're so rude," Elizabeth said. "How did they get away with it?"

"It's art," I explained. "This was called Rubens' Rest. And Rubens was famous for his paintings of nude women."

"They're grotesque," Elizabeth said. "And they're enormous. They're like whales."

"I don't think Welsh people are particularly fat," I said.

"I meant the large sea animals." Elizabeth paused. It sometimes took a while for her to catch on. "Oh, very funny – not," she said.

"Anyway, that was the fashion then. Thin women were considered ugly. You had to be voluptuous to be beautiful. I've read about it."

"What, in a book?"

"I do read books."

"Only if they have pictures in them."

"Comic books are just as important as proper books," I insisted. "They're called graphic novels. And this was a book about art, anyway – so of course it had pictures in it."

The café eating area was about eight metres wide by ten metres long. As you came in through the main door, the pictures covered the long wall opposite and the wall to the right. There were none on the left wall behind the serving counter and the hatch, or around the door to the PGR and the rest of the house.

The paintings had been done rather well. The artist hadn't kept the soft textures of the originals by Rubens, though. He'd gone for a more cartoony feel, a bit like old-fashioned seaside postcards.

"Well, I think they're gross," Elizabeth said. "No wonder the café closed. They're enough to put anyone off their food. And the sooner you paint over them, the better. I don't know what Mum and Dad would think."

"Dad would like them."

"Well, Mum definitely wouldn't. All those fat bottoms everywhere."

"Still, there's one good thing," I said.

"What's that?"

"They make you look thin."

"Oh, thank you very much." Elizabeth looked upset and I knew I should have kept my mouth shut.

"Anyway, I'll paint over them tomorrow. We'll have to paint the walls white first. It might take a couple of coats," I said.

There was a bang on the half-open door.

"Hellooo!"

"Oh dear," Elizabeth said softly. "Another visitor."

17
Front Page Story

A large woman about half the size of a jumbo jet, dressed in motorbike leathers and holding a crash helmet, stood in the doorway.

"Hello, my dears," the woman said. "Is your mother in?"

"I'm afraid we're closed," I said.

She ignored me. "Silver will be OK there for a bit, won't he?" she said.

"Silver?"

"My moped." She pushed past us and put her helmet on a table.

"But it's red," I said.

"I named it after the Lone Ranger's horse."

"Er . . . we *are* closed," Elizabeth said. "And our mother's out shopping at the moment."

The woman was struggling with her leather jacket, which was too small for her. At last she pulled it off and dumped it on a table with her helmet. She was wearing a tweedy suit underneath.

"Our mother doesn't like us talking to strangers,"

Elizabeth continued.

"And quite right too," the woman said, wiping her sweaty face on her sleeve. "Luckily, I'm not a stranger. I'm Mrs Ems." She handed Elizabeth a business card. "From the *Town Crier*. I'm the editor."

"The *Town Crier*," Elizabeth said. "I've seen that in the newsagent's."

"I'd like to run a story about you," Mrs Ems said. "When are you planning to open?"

"August Bank Holiday weekend," I said. "Probably on the Saturday. We're having a grand opening."

"That's next week, isn't it?"

"Yes it is, "Elizabeth said. "We're working really hard to get it finished in time."

"Will there be cream cakes?"

"This *is* a café," I said. "So it's highly likely. It's not unusual to find cakes on a café menu."

"Don't mind my brother," Elizabeth said. "He didn't take his politeness pills today."

"I'm not supposed to eat cream cakes," Mrs Ems went on, "but I make a bit of an exception for special occasions. So, yes, I'd be happy to come."

I gave Elizabeth a look which said: I don't remember inviting her.

Elizabeth gave me a strange look back which said:

Why are you looking at me so strangely?

"Yes, do come," Elizabeth said. "We are planning quite a spread."

Mrs Ems was gazing around the room. "You've cleaned this place up a treat. I used to come here a lot. It was just round the corner from our office back then. We've moved now. What do you think of the nudes, then?"

"Not a lot," Elizabeth said. "We're going to paint over them. Wilf is going to paint something a bit more modern."

"Wilf?"

"That's me," I said. "I'm an artist."

"Like Rubens?"

"Well," I said. "Not quite as famous."

"Not yet," Mrs Ems said and winked. "But you might be one day, eh? Be a shame to see those nudes go. They don't make women like that any more. Of course, they didn't have diets in those days."

I looked at Mrs Ems. She was as big as the women on the walls. If she took her clothes off. . . Oh dear, I wished I hadn't thought of that.

"You could do some nice pictures of food. Big French sticks. Maybe some grapes trailing round the room," she said.

"I'm going to do comic-book heroes," I said.

"Oh, yes." For an editor writing a story about us, she didn't seem terribly interested. "I don't suppose you've got a cup of tea on the go?" she asked.

"Not really," I said.

"I think we could find you one," Elizabeth said. "We're just about done for today."

"That would be great, my dears. And I don't suppose you've got any cakes? Or biscuits, even?"

"I'll see," Elizabeth said.

"A chocolate digestive would go down a treat. I'm allowed something nice once in a while." Mrs Ems rummaged in her bag and produced a tiny camera. "I'll just take a few snaps, if that's OK."

Briony appeared. "Wow! So that's what's been hiding under all those years of dirt."

"Good afternoon," Mrs Ems said. "I'm from the *Town Crier*. We're going to run a feature on you. And you are. . . ?"

"Briony."

"And I didn't ask your sister's name. I must write this down." She searched in her pockets, produced a notepad and a pencil, and began asking questions. We told her as much as we could. The publicity would be just what we needed.

"So, there are five of you children," she said, when we'd finished. "And I expect you'll all help in the café when it's open. A real family affair, eh?"

"That's right," Elizabeth said, appearing with the refreshments.

"I bet your mum and dad are proud of you all."

"I wouldn't be surprised," I said.

And so, after some more chat and questions, Mrs Ems got up to go. "I suppose you know all about the last owner."

"Not a lot," Elizabeth said.

"Nice chap. He was an artist. He painted the walls. John Montague, his name was. Some of the locals were up in arms. There were quite a lot of complaints. They thought the paintings were in very bad taste. The *Crier* defended Montague. If you can't paint giant nudes on your own walls, where can you paint them?"

"Where indeed?" I said enigmatically.

"Well," she went on. "The thing was . . . he disappeared. Suddenly. Quite a mystery, it was. He didn't tell anyone where he was going. Or that he was going. All his clothes and possessions were found in the house after he'd gone. And the fridge was full of food. Rather suspicious."

"Like the *Marie Celeste*," Briony said. "They found it

drifting with no crew. A ghost ship."

"This is a house of mysteries, isn't it," I said. "Like the murder in the cellar."

Mrs Ems creased her brow. "A murder? I don't remember anything about a murder."

"It happened hundreds of years ago," I said. "Mrs Herring told us. That's why the house is haunted."

"Well, how about that? I didn't know there'd been a murder here. And I didn't know it was haunted," Mrs Ems said, glancing at her watch. "Goodness me. Look at the time. Must rush." At the door she peered up at the sky. "Looks like it might rain."

"Glory be," I said. "Rain? That would be . . . er . . . unusual."

"Our weather person said it would rain and she's hardly ever wrong. She's very nice, our weather person. Bakes her own bread. She's got one of those portable ovens. And she makes lovely scones."

We watched as she grabbed the moped propped up against the window. "Tell your parents I was here. And don't forget to buy a copy of the *Town Crier* on Friday. Bye!"

Holding the machine firmly and with a cry of "Hi-Ho Silver, away!" Mrs Ems ran, pushing the moped, jumped on and started to pedal furiously. She lurched to the left, but caught her balance just as the moped spluttered into life. She revved the tiny engine, wobbled a couple of times for good luck and bounced up the road in a cloud of smoke.

"Well," Elizabeth said. "What about that!"

"Looks like the exhaust needs repairing," I said.

"No," Elizabeth said. "I mean, about John Montague. The last owner of this place. Fancy him going missing."

"I wonder," Briony mused, "why the editor came round in person. I mean, why didn't she just send a reporter?"

"The lure of cream cakes, I suspect," I said.

"Or biscuits," Elizabeth added. "She ate the whole packet."

"And you'd have thought the local paper would have known about the murder," Briony said. "Well, I'm going to take a few more pictures for the scrapbook. Everybody – smile!"

18
The Sound of Music

I got up early. (Don't faint! I can get up before midday if I really have to.) And today we were going to paint the walls white. I contemplated having a wash, but as I'd only be getting covered in paint, there didn't seem much point.

Sammi was up early too. I found her in the yard fiddling with the Gerald trap. "You won't catch him," I told her.

"I will. I'm going to use fish fingers. No one can resist fish fingers."

"Are they the ones that have been in the fridge for a couple of weeks? Won't they be off?"

Sammi sniffed them. "They do smell a bit whiffy. But Gerald will probably like that."

I went into the shed and looked around. It was piled high with old boxes, paint cans with brushes glued into them with hard paint, and broken furniture. A mattress was propped against one wall. Everything was damp and mouldy and there was a smell of rotting wood and mildew. I wondered how many spiders lived there.

I peered into the top of a wooden crate and gingerly hooked out an old slide projector. I'd seen one just like it at school. They used them before computers were invented. Maybe there were some slides somewhere. We could have a slide show – that would be fun.

But upon closer inspection, the projector turned out to be rusted up. If it was turned on it would probably electrocute someone or start a fire. It looked to be beyond repair. I was about to drop it back into the crate when I noticed there was still a slide loaded in the holder. I took it out. It might prove interesting. I let the projector fall back into the box.

Then I noticed some picture frames poking out from above the back of a smelly sofa. I asked Sammi to give me a hand, but she refused, on the grounds that the sofa was stinky and covered in bird poo. Well, she had a point.

It took a while shifting everything about, but at last I managed to retrieve the frames. I had to be careful not to disturb the spiders. They were in fact oil paintings. There were three – and I recognised them. I'd seen them in the art gallery. One was a copy of the Kandinsky I really liked, a big smeary picture of a train, all bright colours and splodges of paint. It was a good copy, too. The artist had obviously spent some time doing it. Another was of the Red Square painting that the art gallery attendant had sniffed at. The third was an impressionistic picture of a woman sitting at a table eating something – I couldn't quite see what, because the paintings were covered in white mould and spotted with something black and smelly.

I guessed they'd been painted by John Montague. He was an art critic and the newspaper woman had said he was an artist, so he must have done them. It was a shame they were in such a bad way.

I was wondering whether they'd be worth restoring and hanging on the café walls, when I heard music. Someone had fixed the radio. That would have to be Briony. I don't know if I've mentioned it, but Briony's a bit of a genius. She doesn't get it from Mum or Dad, I'm sure. Dad's very bright, but he can only *just* manage to make a cup of coffee.

I laid the paintings carefully against the wall, stepped gingerly over Sammi's rat trap and made my way indoors. I didn't think much of Briony's choice of music. I didn't know that The Cure had covered that old Sex Pistols' song, "My Way" – and featuring a saxophone, too.

The music made me think. We'd need music in the

café. A juke box would be good. A juke box would fit in well with the comics theme. I'd get Briony to have a look on eBay. We could find loads of old Sixties records, and even some Cure. Not Amber Lite, though. I'd have to draw the line at that.

The PGR was empty and so was the kitchen. I followed the music into the café and there were Elizabeth, Jaz, Briony, Sammi and Killer, all staring out of the window.

In the street, with his back to us, was the mad busker. The noise he was making was alarming. He'd never be short of work on a ferry – warning other boats in the fog!

"You're up, then," Elizabeth said to me.

"Of course I am," I said. "I've been up ages."

"It's the mad busker," said Briony.

"What I don't understand," Elizabeth said, "is why he's here. No one comes down this street unless they're coming here."

"Or going to the lock shop," Jaz said.

"Ask him to stop," Sammi said. "He's frightening Kevin."

"I don't think he is," I said. Killer was sitting on the counter by the window staring intently at the busker's back as if he were a large and particularly tasty bird.

"Maybe we should set Killer onto him. That would scare him off," Briony said.

"Ask him to go away," Elizabeth said to me. "It's giving me a headache."

"Me? Why me?" I asked.

"Because you're a man," said Elizabeth. "It's a man's job."

"I'm not a man," I said. "I'm a boy. And anyway, it's not a man's job."

"Yes it is," Jaz said. "Like washing up and doing the ironing. It's in the rule book. Rule 27. Telling buskers to shut up."

"That's the old rule book," I said. "In the new edition which only came out yesterday, Rule 27 says that I can designate someone else to tell buskers to shut up. And I designate you. And anyway, I'm painting in here today. It might be nice to have some musical accompaniment."

"Well, it's up to you," Jaz said. "I'm off to meet Kavita and Sandy."

"Great," I said, sarcastically. "We're going to spend all day painting, working on the café and getting it ready for Mum and Dad, and you're going out to play with your friends, sitting about drinking Cokes and eating ice cream and having a good time."

"Well, as a matter of fact, smarty-pants," Jaz said, "we're going to be working too. We're going to plan some recipes for the café. Kavita and Sandy are going to help. They've got to do a holiday project for school and that's what it's going to be. They've got some really good ideas. And I'm going to work out how I can cook everything."

"That's wonderful," Elizabeth said.

"What do you say?" Jaz said, staring at me.

Oh dear. I shouldn't have flown at Jaz like that. Mum was always telling me to keep my mouth under control. My mouth has a habit of running away with me.

"Well?" Jaz said again.

"I'm sorry," I said. "I'm very, very, very sorry."

"I should think so," Jaz said.

"I'm sooooorrrrrrrrryyyyyyyyyy. . ." I started singing and swaying and waving my arms in the air to the music coming from outside. "So sooooorrrrrrryyyyyyyyyyyy... pleeeeease forgiiiiiiiiiiiiive meeeeeee. . ."

"OK, OK, OK," Jaz said, "No need to make a song and dance about it."

"The music," Elizabeth said. "It's stopped."

We looked out of the big window, and there was

the mad busker staring back at us. He was mouthing something.

"What's he saying?" Sammi asked.

"I think he wants to know if we have any requests," Briony said.

"Ask him if he can play 'Over the Hills and Far Away'," Jaz said.

"Who's that by?" Sammi asked.

"Oasis," I said.

I went over to the café doors, unlocked them and threw them open. Clean, salty air flooded in and the sound of seagulls echoed through the skies.

"Hello, laddie," the busker said. "Thought I'd pay you a visit – see how you were getting on. Here." He handed me the saxophone and stepped in. "They call me Ironhead," he said. "Och, look at them." He indicated the pictures on the wall. "They've scrubbed up well. Caused a bit of a stir, they did. Course, everyone soon got used to them. Good publicity and all that."

"We're going to paint over them," Elizabeth said.

"Shame. What are you going to put in their place?"

"Comic book heroes," I said.

"Nah. You should do some bands. Deep Purple on that wall, Ozzy Osbourne on that one."

Elizabeth introduced everyone, and asked, "Would you like a cup of tea?"

"That would go down a treat," Ironhead said.

"I think we'll be OK for customers when we open," I said. "We seem to have quite a few already."

"Well, I'm off," Jaz said.

While Elizabeth made the tea and Briony and Sammi chatted to our new musical friend, I busied myself getting the paint together. We'd bought three giant tins of white emulsion in a sale, some big brushes and rollers. The walls shouldn't be too difficult.

By the time I was ready to start, Ironhead was ready to go. "Reckon the weather's going to brighten up later," he said. "I'll probably try the seafront. Usually make a bit there."

"Why are you called Ironhead?" I asked him.

"Good question. Is it that (a) I have an iron head? (b) I was once in a heavy metal band called Iron Head? (c) My surname is Ironhead? (d) All three?"

"Isn't that four?" Briony asked.

"Could it be two out of the three?" I queried.

"Where's my sax?" broke in Ironhead.

We all looked around. The large instrument was no longer propped up by the door where I'd put it.

"There it is," Sammi squealed, and rushed across

the room. "Naughhhty pussy. Put it down." Killer had the strap in his claws and was dragging the instrument behind the serving counter. Killer growled, but let Sammi retrieve it.

"It's heavy," she said.

"It ain't heavy," he said, "it's my brother's."

Elizabeth and Sammi looked at him blankly. "A hit by The Hollies," I said. "A Sixties band."

"We weren't born then," Elizabeth said to him, "so we're not likely to get that reference."

"Your brother did."

"Yeah, but he's a pop nerd."

Ironhead took the sax from Sammi.

"What kind of sax is it?" I asked.

"It's a tenor."

"I'd have thought it would cost much more than that," I said.

Everyone fell about laughing – well, not exactly. But some jokes deserve a little outing from The Old Jokes' Rest Home now and again. Dad would have been proud.

19
Ladies in Coats

It took us until mid-afternoon to finish the first coat of paint. The naked ladies were still showing through. It would take about twenty more coats, I reckoned. Especially to cover their bottoms, which were very big. Did women really have such massive bottoms in those days?

Briony had decided to lend a hand, too. Maybe she'd felt guilty when I had a go at Jaz. But she'd been doing a very important job – looking after the money and budgeting so that we had enough to buy the paint and the other things we needed. Not to mention ordering all the food and other stuff online, setting up our website and designing the menus.

Even Sammi helped with the decorating, painting the low bits she could reach. And as we painted, we chatted about the forthcoming opening of the café. Would we be able to do it in time? Everything did seem to be taking twice as long as it should and there was just over a week to go. We talked about Mum and Dad, about whether the break would help them shout at one another less. (We'd had another card from Mum, by the way.) And we talked about the owner, John Montague, and why he'd disappeared.

"The café was probably losing money," I suggested, "and so he got into debt and then committed suicide by jumping off the end of the pier."

"Or maybe he was on the pier," Sammi said, "and his hat blew off. So he jumped in the water after it and drowned."

"There is no pier," Elizabeth said.

I sighed. "I expect it got washed away in all the rain!"

"Oh no," Sammi gasped. "Maybe he died, and it's his ghost we can hear."

"No, it's not!" Briony said sharply.

"He was an interesting character, I bet," I said. "He painted the walls in here. And I've found some paintings he did – copies of pictures in the art gallery."

"It is intriguing, though, isn't it," Briony said, "why he disappeared. I think I'll do some digging. See what I can find out."

As soon as we'd finished the painting, Briony vanished upstairs and Sammi left on some secret mission, probably involving Gerald and an even more elaborate rat trap. Killer was nowhere to be seen. In fact, we hadn't seen him since the lid came off the first can of paint. Obviously a cat with very delicate nostrils.

The door banged open and cold, wet air blew in.

"Hello again."

It was Frank of Frank Meek Motors (Antique). And he had a dog with him. A German Shepherd. It looked a bit mangy.

I glanced around to make sure Killer was nowhere to be seen. The last thing we wanted was Frank's dog getting hurt.

"Hello, I'm Frank. Remember me?"

"Of course I remember you," I said, shaking his outstretched hand. "You sell cars. Your name is Frank."

"I remember you, too."

"They're a great band," I said.

"Who?"

"No," I said, "not The Who. They were a 60s band. U2".

"Ah. . ." Frank looked confused. As well he might.

"I meant, I remember you as well. Not the band. . . I never forget a face. I've a long memory. You should remember that."

"I won't forget."

"I was just passing and thought I'd look in. This is Prints." The dog glared at me with big, baleful eyes. I bent to stroke him. He growled.

"Don't touch him," Frank said. "He gets very nervous. I don't suppose he'll bite your hand off, but you don't want to go risking it."

I withdrew my hand sharply. The dog growled again, and a dribble of spittle rolled down his chin and plopped onto the floor.

"Friends of ours had a dog called Prince," Elizabeth said.

"Yeah, well, Prints is spelt P-R-I-N-T-S. When he was a puppy, he walked through a pool of blood and left footprints everywhere. The name kind of stuck."

"*Yeuch!*" Elizabeth pulled a face.

"A pool of blood?" I said.

"There had been a . . . well . . . an accident, shall we say. Best not to go there."

"That's fine by me," I said.

"So," Frank said to Elizabeth, "have we met before?"

"I don't think so. I'm Elizabeth."

"My name's Frank. Frank Meek of Frank Meek Motors (Antique)."

"Mum's out," I said. "She's having her hair done."

"Nice." Frank gazed round the room. "You found the fat ladies, then. I'm not surprised you're painting over them. They're not to everyone's taste."

"Certainly not mine," Elizabeth said.

"You want pictures of cars," Frank said. "I've got a Bugatti in the garage. A picture of that would look sweet on the big wall opposite the door. You could put an Aston Martin Sports over there. And I'm doing up a Triumph Dolomite at the moment. . ."

"I'm going to paint comic-book heroes," I said.

"We could do an advertising deal. You could put some of my cars on your walls. "

"Sorry," I said. "Definitely superheroes."

"You could have them driving cars. . ."

I shook my head.

"Or have cars in the background. . ."

"No."

"Ah, well. If you change your mind. . . Did you tell your mum I'd called?"

"Of course," I said. "She says she doesn't want a car, thank you very much. And Dad's got one already."

"Maybe he'd like two?"

"He's getting a motorbike, actually."

"Ah . . . well . . . this could be his lucky day. It so happens. . ."

Our conversation was interrupted by a low growling noise. Prints was straining on his lead and spraying spittle everywhere. Then a terrible high-pitched wail came from the dining-room doorway. Prints had spotted Killer. And Killer had spotted Prints. Now the fur was going to fly. And probably lots more spittle.

"Maybe you'd better go," I said, "just to be on the safe side."

"Maybe you're right," Frank said, dragging Prints towards the door. "Prints is very fond of cats."

"That's nice," Elizabeth said.

"Yeah. Nothing he likes better than chewing on a tasty cat bone. Heh, heh. Tell your folks I called."

Killer ambled nonchalantly across the room to the door and peered down the road after them. Then he drew a pistol from his holster and aimed at the retreating dog, fired, blew imaginary smoke from the barrel, twirled it twice in his paw and, in one deft motion, slid it back into his holster.

"I didn't like the look of him," Elizabeth said. "I wonder what he wanted."

I shrugged. "He wants to sell Mum and Dad a new car. Salesmen like him never give up. He'll be round again."

"Well, I hope he leaves the dog at home next time."

I nodded in agreement. "Come on. Let's get tidied up."

Elizabeth gathered up the brushes and rollers and disappeared into the kitchen. I was about to follow, when there was a bang on the window and the door swung open again. We should open the café now, I thought. We'd do a roaring trade.

It was Ironhead. "Brought you this," he said, and handed me a CD. "Our old band. Iron Head. Do you like heavy metal?"

"It's OK," I said.

"The album's called *Zinc Alloy Feet*. The original was on vinyl. Had it transferred. It's digital now. Everything's digital these days, isn't it?"

I nodded.

"I played guitar then. That's me." He pointed to a much younger and longer-haired version of himself on the cover. "Maybe you could sell a few in the café when it opens."

"I don't know," I said. "It's not going to be a record shop, is it?"

"Well, some cafés hang pictures on the walls that you can buy, don't they? You could have a picture of Iron Head on the wall. Then you could sell their music. I've still got a few CDs. And there are still some fans about. Anyway, ask your mum."

"I will," I said. "But I don't think she's a heavy metal fan."

"I say a few CDs," Ironhead said, "but actually I've got a couple of thousand."

"I'm not sure."

"We could give them away. As a promotion. Is your mum around?"

"No," I said. "She's off having her toenails clipped."

"Women." Ironhead sighed, and then winked. "Mysterious creatures, aren't they?"

I nodded. My sisters certainly were.

"Well, best be off. Enjoy the album."

"I will."

When he'd gone I locked the door. I noticed dog spittle on the floor and wondered if I should clean it up. No point. It would soon dry.

Tonight I would do some work on the designs. Soon I would get to the fun part – putting the artwork on the walls. I was really looking forward to it.

20
More Figments

Vampyre was impatient now. It would soon be dawn. There must be some way into the building below. It raised its huge clawed foot and brought it down on the roof with all the force it could muster. A great hole appeared and broken slates scattered in every direction. Vampyre grinned, and lowered its great bulk into the dark attic space below. It peered around, looking for a way out, and spied the trap door. It stopped and listened. It could hear breathing.

Was there a human sleeping below? Vampyre sniffed the air. It was the smell of human, all right. Vampyre grinned again. Not long now. . .

I opened my eyes and for a moment wondered where I was. I peered into the surrounding blackness. Slowly, my eyes became accustomed to the darkness. There was a creak from somewhere above me, like someone or something heavy shifting its weight from one foot to another. The image of the nightmarish creature creeping across the attic joists came back to me. I shuddered, and glanced at the door. But I knew it was only a dream.

In the background I could hear the soft whistle of wind and the sound of the swell of the sea. I could also make out a faint tapping on the window – the sound of rain, like fingers drumming softly on a tabletop. And then I heard it – that sound again. That low, unearthly whispering. The voice, muffled and contorted by the thickness of the walls and the crying wind. *Murder*, the voice said. *Murder. Murder.*

I shivered. I was scared. But I slid from beneath the duvet, grabbed my shorts and carefully picked my way over the piles of comics and other debris littering my floor. I followed the voice down the stairs. It was coming from Sammi's room.

I pushed the door gently open. There was a muffled shriek that made me jump.

Sammi was sitting up in bed, her duvet pulled around her so that you could just see the top half of her face.

"Oh," she said, "it's you."

"That noise," I said. "I heard it."

She nodded. "It's the ghost. The figment thing. I'm scared."

I sat beside her and put my arm around her, and we listened. We listened for a long time, but the voice had gone. All we could hear was the wind blowing around the chimney tops as it gusted in from the sea, and rain on the window.

"What was it?" Sammi asked.

I listened to the groan of the old house and thought about the murder that had happened hundreds of years ago in the cellar, and wondered about the ghost. Were there such things as ghosts – or was Briony right – ghosts didn't exist?

"Not a ghost," I said. "There's no such thing as ghosts."

"It's the figment, then."

"No . . . a figment is . . . um. . ."

"I think it's the ghost of the artist who lived here. The one who went missing," Sammi said.

"Don't be silly," I said. "Just because the owner of this place disappeared, it doesn't mean he's a ghost. He probably couldn't pay his bills and ran away. Anyway, the ghost is gone now."

"You think the ghost is real, don't you?"

"It's just the wind," I said, "that's all."

"I want Mummy."

I hugged her. "She'll be home next week. That's not long to wait, is it? And won't she be surprised when she finds the café all ready?"

"I miss her."

"I know. We all do."

"OK, I'll try and go back to sleep, shall I?"

"Would you like me to stay here with you?" I asked.

"It's all right. Kevin will look after me."

I looked around. There was no sign of the cat. Sammi pulled the duvet back and there was Killer, curled up beside her.

I smiled. "OK," I whispered, "goodnight."

And I crept from the room. I wasn't sure if sleeping with a maniac cat was such a good idea. Maybe I should have said no. If only Mum were here. She always knew what to do at times like this.

Back in my bed I tried to sleep. But I felt cold and I was still sure I could hear someone – or something – moving around above me. Ghosts really are only figments of our imagination, I told myself. Even so, knowing that didn't seem to help. And it was ages before I fell asleep again.

21
An Inspector Calls

It looked as if the second coat of paint had done the trick, and Elizabeth and I felt pleased with ourselves. You could still see the outline of a bare bottom in places, but by the time I'd painted over the top, they'd be gone. With the kitchen and the café cleaned and this room painted white, I felt as if we were getting somewhere.

We'd packed the paint tins away and were admiring our handiwork, when I became aware of a large figure standing at the door, peering in through the steamy glass. It was a big man in a beige raincoat and a white hat. He banged on the door. He didn't look like the sort of person you'd invite in. He looked as if he'd give even Killer a run for his money.

"What do you think?" I asked Elizabeth. "Should we let him in?"

"See what he wants."

I opened the door. "Sorry," I said. "We're not open yet."

The man felt in his inside pocket and produced

a police identity card. "My name is Inspector Carpet," he said, "and I wondered if I might come in."

I peered at the ID card. You couldn't be too careful. They were always telling us that. I peered at the photo and then at the police officer. "Are you sure it's you?"

"Of course it is. Look!" He pulled a face like the one in the photo – one eyebrow raised and an enigmatic smirk, as if he'd just arrested someone for dropping a crisp packet in the street. "Now let me in."

"You look younger in the photo," I said.

"Just let me in, OK?"

"Come in, then," I said.

"We haven't done anything wrong, have we?" Elizabeth asked.

Inspector Carpet stared at her through lowered eyes. "I don't know if you've done anything wrong. You tell me. Have you done anything wrong?"

"I said a swear word when I dropped my toffee apple on the beach," I said. "That was wrong, wasn't it?"

"That depends on the word. I wondered if it might be possible to speak to your mum or dad."

"I'm afraid they're out," Elizabeth said.

"Yes," I added. "Dad's working in France and Mum's having her weekly abseiling session."

"Abseiling?"

"That's right," I continued. "They climb cliffs and walls. She's going on an expedition to Everest next year. She's going to be the first person to abseil down it."

"That takes me back," Inspector Carpet said.

"Have you climbed Everest, then?" I asked.

The inspector was gazing around the room. "You've painted over those ghastly nudes."

I nodded. "I'm going to do comic book heroes."

"No, no, no," the Inspector said. "What you want are some nice Mediterranean scenes with the sun and the sand and the sea and palm trees waving in the balmy breeze – not that you would see the breeze in a painting, of course." He sighed. "I don't suppose you've a cuppa on the go, have you?"

"I'm sorry," Elizabeth said. "We don't open until the Bank Holiday."

"I saw in the paper that you were doing this place up."

I'd forgotten all about the newspaper feature. "It's in the paper, then?"

"Oh yes," the inspector said. "There's a very nice picture of you two. Well . . . there are five of you, aren't there?" He gazed around the room some more.

"It will be good to have this place open again. Are you absolutely certain that there's no chance of a cup of tea?"

"I'll put the kettle on," Elizabeth said.

The police officer took off his coat and laid it carefully on a table. Then he sat down gingerly. The chair wobbled a bit but held his weight. "This chair's a bit on the tentative side," he said.

"We've ordered some new ones."

"So, what can we do for you?" Elizabeth asked.

"I just thought I might have a word with your folks and ask them if they would like to join Neighbourhood Watch."

"They send an inspector round for that?" I asked.

"Neighbourhood Watch plays a very important part in the detection and prevention of crime, you know."

"I suppose so," I said.

We all sat in silence for a bit.

"You used to come here, then?" I asked him.

"Oh yes," the inspector chuckled grimly. "It wasn't unknown for me to frequent this establishment from time to time."

"Did you know the last owner?"

"We weren't . . . um . . . personally acquainted."

"He disappeared, didn't he?" Elizabeth said.

"He did, as a matter of fact. There was some conjecture that he had run away with a woman, and I have to say that I wouldn't have been surprised. Mind you, he left all his belongings behind and, as I said to my wife at the time, no woman's worth that, if you know what I mean. And the paperwork that case involved was amazing. Great times, they were. I used to *like* the paperwork. Not everybody did, but it came natural to me, like breathing, or sleeping after a heavy meal."

There was another silence while Elizabeth made the tea. I was hoping that we might learn a bit more about this place and its owner but Inspector Carpet didn't seem very inclined to talk further about it. I thought I'd try a different tack.

"Is it exciting in the police force?" I asked.

"It can be. Lots of administration. Lots of forms to fill in. Lots of paperwork. It's not all car chases and shoot-outs, you know."

"There was a big robbery in the town once, though, wasn't there? From the art gallery. Some Russian icons were stolen, weren't they?"

"That's right. I worked on that case, as a matter of fact. The icons were big news at the time. The gallery had acquired six of them. Six Russian icons. Quite a coup. And then they were stolen. We got the culprit, though."

"So what happened?" I asked.

"Let me see. It was a few years ago. As I remember it, the thief got into the gallery late at night. Without setting off the alarms, which was odd. But, as luck would have it, one of our lads was walking past the gallery at the time. He was on night duty. Young constable. Now, what was his name? Ah, yes – Robbie. Nice young man. He noticed a suspicious-looking car parked outside the town hall – and as soon as he started to walk towards it, the car drove off. Next minute, the thief's at the top of the gallery steps, sees our chap looking up at him and makes a run for it. Robbie gives chase and catches him. Art thief apprehended. Simple as that. Robbie was a bit of a hero." The inspector sipped his tea. "You make a good cuppa," he told Elizabeth.

"Thanks," Elizabeth said.

"We suspected it was an inside job," the inspector went on, "And the car turned out to be stolen – Robbie'd got the registration number – so there was at least one other person involved. But the thief wouldn't say who it was. He went to prison and that was that. Job done." The inspector sighed. "Anyway, I must be off. Please be so kind as to tell your mum and dad I called about Neighbourhood Watch. Here, let me give you this." He felt in his pocket and produced a card. It said:

Bob Odd Job
DIY. Gardening. Decorating
No job too small.

And there was a phone number.

"I thought you were a police officer," I said.

"I am. Although I'm semi-retired now, of course."

"Semi-retired?"

"Yes, that's correct. I help with Neighbourhood Watch, obviously, and I go into the station on Mondays, Wednesdays and every other Thursday to help with the paperwork. These young officers you get nowadays, they've no idea about paperwork. We had great paperwork in the old days. We used to get through reams and reams of the stuff. It's all computers now."

The inspector pulled his coat on. "Well, that was a very nice cup of tea. And tell your mum, good luck with the abseiling."

22
Rumbled

Saturday. After breakfast we held a meeting. We'd had a card from Mum saying she'd booked a flight for Saturday, August 27th. There was much whooping and cheering. Sammi and Jaz, in particular, were missing her a lot, I could tell. Call it boy's intuition; and the fact that they'd dressed the shop-window dummy in Mum's clothes and sat it in Mum's place at the PGR table. I wasn't sure that her pink top went with her orange scarf, but Jaz said it was the fashion. None of it went with the pukey green walls.

"That's good, then," I said. "Mum comes back on Saturday 27th. That's one week today. We can make that the official opening day for The Comic Café."

"Only a week," Elizabeth said. "And there's still so much to do."

"I reckon we can do it in a week," Jaz said. "Kavita and Sandy have got everything organised kitchen-wise. And Kavita's got some brilliant Indian recipes, too."

"And won't it be a surprise for Mum," Briony said.

"Mum's coming home," Sammi shouted. "Wheeeeeeeeeeeeee!"

But with only one week to go, it was going to be hard work. I was to design a poster which Briony would print and Jaz and her friends would distribute around the town. That would take care of the advertising.

Elizabeth was going to help Briony order the food and drink and get all that sorted out, once Jaz and the girls worked out exactly what they'd need. She was also going to ask Thumbs, our electrician friend opposite, to check all the wiring and electrical stuff in the kitchen.

My main task was to finish the painting. The walls hadn't dried very well and needed another coat of white paint. You could still see the bottoms quite clearly, now that the paint had dried. Perhaps it had been a mistake buying cheap emulsion. But we were running out of money. We all agreed to look on the internet for some better paint to finish off the walls. We knew we'd have to use mum's credit card, but we decided it would be worth it.

As well as doing the artwork on the walls, I had to paint the name over the shopfront. With only seven days left, I was wondering if we'd do it in time.

We talked about the police officer's visit.

"I think Neighbourhood Watch is a great idea," Elizabeth said. "I expect Mum and Dad will want to sign up."

"He was involved in the robbery at the art gallery," I told Briony, Jaz and Sammi, who hadn't met Inspector Carpet.

"Wow!" said Sammi. "Do you mean a police officer stole the painting?"

"No. I mean he was involved in the investigation. He said there was probably someone who worked for the gallery involved, and a third person who drove the car."

"John Montague worked for the gallery didn't he?" Elizabeth said.

"That's interesting," Briony said. "Yes he did."

"It's more likely to be a Russian mastermind," I said, "trying to get their paintings back!"

"Did the police officer say anything about John Montague going missing?" Briony asked.

I shook my head. "Not really. He said he might have run off with a woman. But that's unlikely, because he left all his stuff behind. Did I tell you I found some of his paintings?"

"Was the police officer an artist too?" Jaz said.

"No, Dumbo! I mean John Montague's paintings.

They were in the shed. They're in a bit of state, but they might clean up."

"I was joking," Jaz said. "And don't call me a large Disney character!"

"What shall I call you then? How about Shrek-breath?"

"Stop it," Elizabeth said.

"Yes," said Sammi, "stop arguing. Be happy. Mum's coming home. Just one more week! Hurrah!"

"Hello, everyone," said Mrs Herring.

We all stopped talking, turned and stared at her. She must have let herself in. I should have locked the café door. I wondered how much she'd heard.

"How are you all?" she asked.

"Er . . . fine," Elizabeth said.

"Vere's your mum?"

"Here she is," Sammi said, pointing at the dummy. "Can't you see her?"

"She's had to go to her astronaut class," I said.

"Astronaut class?"

"Yes, she's training to be the next woman in space."

"That's right," Briony agreed. "Last week she did weightlessness and today they're practising eating food through a toothpaste tube."

"And floating," I said. "That's very important, knowing how to float properly. If you can't float, you—"

"She's not here!" Mrs Herring interrupted. "She's not been here all along. Neizer has your dad! I know zis!"

". . . bump into things," I said lamely.

There was a silence. This one was long – one of those silences where everyone looks at one another and you desperately want to say something but don't know what. We'd been rumbled.

In the end, it was Elizabeth who spoke.

"Mum and Dad are on holiday."

"Zat's disgraceful," Mrs Herring said. "Zey vent on holiday and left you all on your own? I've good mind to report zem to authorities."

"But it wasn't like that," Elizabeth went on, "they both decided to have a holiday at the same time, but didn't tell one another."

"I'm not quite viz you," Mrs Herring said.

Elizabeth explained, with us adding bits from time to time just to make it even more confusing.

"Mum's coming home next Saturday," Sammi said.

"That's right," I said. "That's why we're going to open the café then. It's going to be a big surprise.

She doesn't know anything about it."

"I see," Mrs Herring said, when we'd finished trying to explain. Then she smiled. "Vell . . . how about cup of tea, da?" And she joined us at the table.

"I'll make a fresh pot," Elizabeth said.

"Vot amazing children. And you've got just vone veek. Do you zink you can do it in time?"

"We think we can," I said.

"Could I help? It sounds like you'll need plenty of help. I am qualified cleaner."

"And you won't tell anyone about Mum and Dad?" Briony said.

"Of course not. Don't vorry. Your secret's safe viz me."

So that was that. Mrs Herring was on board. There was something odd about her and I admit that at first I didn't feel I could trust her. But maybe I was wrong. You can't not trust someone just because she has thin lips, can you?

And so the café opening was official and we were ready to go. The next seven days were going to be very interesting indeed.

23
Say Hi to Superman

Sunday morning. But not for me a long-lie in and a cup of tea in bed. Nor a relaxed stroll along the seafront to watch the brass band playing the best of Amber Lite on the bandstand. No. While most people were reading the Sunday papers over a plate of scrambled eggs, sausages and mushrooms, I was working, standing on a chair that was balanced on a table, drawing the outline of Spiderman with a charcoal pencil.

I could have done with a lie-in, mind. After Mrs Herring had gone we'd found some better quality white paint on the internet and gone to pick it up. Then we'd spent the evening giving the walls yet another coat. This time it worked. The fat bottoms had finally disappeared.

I'd decided to draw a scene from a Spiderman comic across the back wall – that's the long wall that faces you as you come in through the café door – tt's the wall you see first. Then, for the wall to the right, I'd decided on the X-Men. And on the left, on the wall behind the counter, high up, Superman flying through the air clutching a baguette.

It meant no Batman and no Incredible Hulk but, well, that couldn't be helped. I'd decided against werewolves and vampires. I'd been tempted to go for minor characters but I didn't want to confuse the general public who, I think, are probably quite conservative when it comes to superheroes. And, anyway, Michelangelo probably missed out loads of cherubs and angels when he did the Sistine Chapel.

The painting took me all day. I must say, I thought it would be quicker. But when you think that Michelangelo took four years to paint one ceiling and I only took a day to draw on three walls – then that wasn't too bad. And you might ask yourself who was the better artist – me or Michelangelo.

For anyone technically minded, you might like to know that I was using matt emulsion paint. We'd bought big tins of Vesuvius Red, Adriatic Blue, Mellow Yellow, Putting Green, Satsuma Orange and Deep Purple, a tin of Sooty Black for the outlines and a huge tin of Snow White. And some good-quality brushes.

In the evening I designed the posters and explained to Briony how I wanted them to look. She was going to scan my drawings into the computer and add the lettering to them on screen. We'd decided on a hundred posters. That should bring people in.

It was late by the time I'd finally cleared all my comics and old clothes and sketchbooks and pens from my bed and climbed in. My arms ached. In fact, my whole body ached from all the stretching and balancing. When Michelangelo finally finished the Sistine Chapel ceiling, he'd seriously injured his back. I hoped that wouldn't happen to me.

I was soon asleep. No ghosts to wake me, either. Just a sunny Elizabeth with a cup of tea at half-past seven. *Half-past seven?* This was worse than being back at school. I did say a few unpleasant things to Elizabeth, but apologised afterwards. Elizabeth, as always, forgave me. She said she would like to go to Australia one day but would probably use normal transport. And that I was too old to be using the word "poo"!

24
Painting by Numbers

Five days to go, and still so much to do. But the walls were finally prepared for my work of art and Elizabeth and Mrs Herring were primed and ready to go.

I don't know if you've ever seen those pictures made from do-it-yourself painting-by-numbers kits. The idea is that the picture is divided up into hundreds of shapes and each shape is given a number to correspond with its colour. So you paint all the shapes numbered 1 in red, number 2 blue, number 3 green, and so on. This is how we had decided to paint our superhero walls. I had drawn all the outlines and written in a number so that everyone knew what colours they had to be. As well as the regular colours, I'd also prepared light and dark versions, mixing the colours with white or black, and so we ended up with twenty shades and twenty numbers. Clever, eh?

The painting went well, and by late morning the room looked very different. Superman's body was now flying across one wall and Spiderman's faceless form flew across another. And the smell was lovely.

I love the smell of paint. There's something about it. It reminds me of Dad and when I was little. He had a box of paints that he kept in the garden shed and I would create fantastic pictures of spaceships and lunar landscapes while he pottered about organising tins of nails and trying to fix things.

Briony appeared with the rough draft of the poster and held it up for everyone's approval.

"You're clever girl," Mrs Herring said.

"Wilf designed it," she said.

"It's teamwork," I explained. "Briony's brilliant on the computer and at working things out. I just get impatient and end up shouting. Basically, I provide the inspiration and Briony turns my vision into the work of art that you see before you."

"Zis whole room, poster, it's amazing. I zink last owner of zis place vould have approved. He vas brilliant artist. Better zan people gave him credit for. And he had quite sense of humour."

"It's not meant to be funny," I said.

"Well, I know what Mrs Herring means," Elizabeth said. "Some things can be serious and funny at the same time. Like you, Wilf. You're always joking, but underneath, you're a very serious person."

Very true, I thought. I made a few suggestions

to improve the poster design, just tiny things, and Briony disappeared to work on the final version. She reckoned she'd have it finished by mid-afternoon and then she and Sammi were off round the town to persuade shops to put the posters in their windows and to find other places to put them up.

Later on, she was going to take some more photos for the *How We Transformed a Derelict Café Into an Amazing Eating Establishment* photo album.

Just before lunch, the first of the big opening day orders from Tesco arrived. I called Jaz, and she and Kavita and Sandy sorted it out.

"This is all the food that will keep," Jaz said. "We've asked for the fresh stuff to be delivered one day before."

"That's right," Sandy agreed. "This is tinned peaches, things like that."

"Tinned peaches?" I said. "*Yeuch!*"

"What's wrong with tinned peaches?" Sandy asked. "We have them all the time at home."

"You might, but we don't, "I said.

"Are you saying there's something wrong with my family?" Sandy asked.

"Anyway," Jaz went on, "we've got tinned apricots, tinned strawberries, tinned pineapple, tinned kiwi fruit, tinned mandarin oranges and tinned gooseberries."

"Couldn't you make things with *real* fruit?" I asked.

"There's nothing wrong with tinned fruit," Sandy said.

"You have to have tinned fruit in a seaside café," Jaz added, "it's traditional. And we've devised special surprise desserts with them."

"Like what?" I asked.

"Can't tell you," Kavita said. "They're secret Indian recipes."

"With tinned fruit?"

"Not just tinned fruit," Kavita said.

"Not that you'll appreciate them," Sandy added.

"Hello, everyone." It was Thumbs, carrying a holdall brimming with tools. "Who have we here, then?"

Elizabeth introduced everyone. "And this is Mrs Herring," she said.

"Pleased to meet you," he said, and shook her hand. He glanced round the room and nodded. "It's looking good, looking good. Superheroes, eh? Didn't like the arty ladies, then?"

"No," Elizabeth said.

"Now, I know what might have worked well –

old-fashioned wallpaper. Red flock. It has a lovely soft feel – like velvet. You see it in Indian restaurants a lot."

"Well, we decided on superheroes," I said.

"If you change your mind . . . I've got a mate in the trade. He can get any wallpaper you want. Dirt cheap."

"That's good to know," I said.

"Yeah, dirt cheap. Mind you, superheroes is OK. But no Doctor Lock? He was my favourite. He could break in anywhere. Fort Knox . . . Tower of London. . ."

"You know a bit about comics, then?" I said. Doctor Lock was pretty obscure.

"Oh yeah, I was a big fan when I was younger, Wilf. A big fan. So . . . do you reckon you'll get it all finished in time?"

"I hope so," I said.

"I'd best get on, then. I should have all the wiring checked by tonight."

"You're so kind," Elizabeth said.

"It's a pleasure. A pleasure. I don't suppose your mum's around today, is she?"

"No, I'm afraid not," I said. "She's doing her volunteer work."

"That's good," Thumbs said. "Community spirit.

Helping the aged." He glanced at Mrs Herring and grinned.

"Well, actually she's a volunteer for some scientific experiments. She's going to be the first woman to travel back in time."

"You're pulling my leg."

I nodded, and grinned, "Yes I am. It's not time travel at all. They're just trying to find a cure for the common cold."

"Right," Thumbs said. "Good for her. I had a really nasty cold in the winter. Well, must get on. Must get on."

"Do you think you could get the freezer working?" Jaz asked him.

"I'll take a look," Thumbs said. And he followed Jaz into the kitchen. Sandy and Kavita picked up some of the carrier bags of food.

"Don't worry about us," Sandy said, looking at me. "We can manage."

"I'm pleased," I said, "because I'm trying to give my arms a rest."

"I'll make cup of tea, shall I?" Mrs Herring suggested.

"Brilliant," Elizabeth said. "I'm parched. And it will make a nice change – someone else making the tea, for once."

Come half-past three, we decided to call it a day. (There were lots of things we could have called it – a saucepan, a tractor – but a day seemed most appropriate.) We'd made stunning progress on the walls. A few more hours' work in the morning and they'd be finished, I reckoned. Mrs Herring had been a great help. She was quick with a brush but also incredibly neat. Now she'd gone off to keep an appointment at the tanning salon. I expect they were doing brilliant business, what with the terrible weather. You certainly couldn't get a tan on the beach.

We were sitting in the PGR with Thumbs. He'd knocked over his cup of tea and Elizabeth was mopping it up.

"At least it didn't go on the poster," I said.

"It's a great poster," Thumbs said. "That'll get people flocking in."

"I'm pleased with it," Briony said.

"Briony and Sammi are going to go round the town to see if they can get some into the shops," I said.

"I'm going to be the salesperson," Sammi said. "Briony's going to tell me what to say."

"Good idea. Now, don't forget to give the bill for

the work I've done to your mum," Thumbs said. "I've done it cut price."

"We won't," I said. "Thanks."

"Everything's safe now. Yeah, safe. But the place needs completely rewiring, really. That's a big job, mind. Have to talk to your mum and dad about that."

"Would you like another cup of tea?" Elizabeth asked.

"No, ta!" Thumbs said. "Gotta go. Just one other thing. I found an odd switch. That one up there." He pointed to a switch high on the wall by the door to the kitchen. "It's live, but it doesn't seem to do anything. It probably runs to an outside light somewhere. I thought it might be in the yard, but there's no light there. I'll check it out another time."

"Well, thanks for all your work," Elizabeth said, as she saw him out.

"It's a pleasure," Thumbs said. "A pleasure."

"So there we are," I said to my sisters. "Everything's hunky-dory and running on schedule. We'll soon have the posters all around the town and the painting's nearly done. We still have the rat problem, mind. Maybe I'll give the rat-catcher a call in the morning."

"No!" Sammi cried.

"He'll catch him humanely," I said, "and let him go, out in the country somewhere." I had my fingers crossed.

"A job well done," Elizabeth said. "To celebrate, I think I'll have a bath."

"I thought I might go for a walk," I said.

"OK," Elizabeth said. "But don't any of you be too late. We'll get some pizza in for supper to celebrate."

"Chocolate pizza!" Sammi yelled in delight.

"Maybe not chocolate. . ." Elizabeth said.

"Come on! Let's go," Briony said to Sammi. "It's poster time."

"There's one thing," Elizabeth said to me. "The chairs. I thought the new chairs were arriving today."

Elizabeth was right. I'd forgotten about that. I found the warehouse number and gave them a ring. Apparently their van had broken down. I explained to the manager that we were opening on Saturday and that the chairs would have to be painted before then, but he said not to worry. The chairs would be with us by tomorrow or Wednesday at the latest.

25
Unsquare Dance

I wandered through the town. The weather had improved. There was just a light drizzle. And it was good to be breathing in fresh air after all those paint fumes.

There were a lot of charity shops. Plenty for Briony to explore. Treasure troves with chests full of black clothes and old computer games. Lots of cafés, too. None of them doing very brisk business. As usual, my doubts about the whole project surfaced. How I'd love to be back home in Slough with my mates!

Ahead of me I saw Mrs Herring going into a café. I considered following her, then decided against it. As I went past I glanced in, and there she was sitting at the same table as Frank Meek. And they were chatting. They knew one another, then. I wouldn't have thought they had much in common. But it was a small town, after all. Maybe she was after a new car. Something smart and black, resembling the Batmobile.

After a while I found myself back at the art gallery, so I thought I'd have another look round. I didn't meet up with my attendant friend on this occasion, though. Instead, I had a look around the rooms I'd missed the first time. No sign of any Pop Art, no Lichtensteins, which was a shame. And one room had a cement mixer in the middle of it and some bags of cement dumped on the floor. I thought there must be some rebuilding going on – but an attendant told me it was an exhibit, an installation. "The shovel too?" I asked. She nodded. "And the empty crisp packets on the floor," she said.

I had a wander around the gallery shop and looked at the postcards. I bought one of the Kandinsky train and one of the Red Square by Malevich. I thought I'd take another look at the originals before I left. Not just the Kandinsky, but the other pictures that Montague had copied were also by Russian artists. Was that a coincidence, or had Montague had a thing about Russian art? As an art critic, that could have been his speciality, I supposed.

I was standing in front of the Red Square painting when something struck me. I got out the postcard I'd bought and compared the two. There was definitely something not quite right. I looked back at the original. It was peculiar. The square wasn't actually a square. If you looked closely, it was on a slight slant. At first I thought it might be some kind of optical illusion, something to do with the picture not being hung straight, or the gallery walls not being true. The thing was, in the picture on the postcard there was also a slight slant – but it was going the other way.

I chuckled to myself. Whoever took the photo for the postcard had printed it the wrong way round. They probably hadn't noticed. Or, if they had, they had thought nobody else would realise. Well, *I'd* noticed! Who would have thought that such a simple painting as a red square on a plain white background could prove so interesting? Such pleasure from little things – what being an artist was all about! Hey-ho. Time to go home. Pepperoni pizza, here I come.

No pizza. Instead, Jaz had decided to attempt a risotto, to use up some of the rice. To make a risotto you fry some onions, then add the rice to the oil for a couple of minutes to coat each grain, then you add stock (which is a bit like thin soup) and mushrooms or whatever else you're using. You add the liquid slowly, stirring all the time, until the rice is lovely and creamy and cooked. Then you stir in the meat or fish – in this instance, tinned tuna – and you can add grated cheese, too. Sounds pretty straightforward, doesn't it? But not everyone can make a good risotto. And there was no way I was going to tell Jaz that she'd proved this point. She had tried her best, after all. And we did have bags and bags of rice that needed using up. But the splodgy, chewy, watery, lumpy gloop Jaz served up definitely wasn't risotto. It was more like that stuff you mix up at school to make papier mâché. It was gruesome.

Jaz was really upset at her culinary disaster and so we played cards, despite being so tired, and let Jaz win. The family that plays together stays together. Well, that wasn't quite right with both Mum and Dad gone. But *we* children were all together – and working well. Maybe we could set up in business. Café Conversions. We convert your pile of rubble into a modern, working café.

Later, I lay in bed and listened to the wind rattling the windows. The postcard I'd bought at the gallery was now pinned up on the wall by my bed. I'd shown the others, but only Briony had shown any interest.

There was a gale blowing up. You could hear the

waves crashing on the beach. There was going to be a high tide tonight. I thought back. Yes, today had been a good day. And first thing next morning, I planned to call the council to get the rat-catcher in.

But, as it happened, the rat-catcher's services were not required. . .

26
Death by Flooding

The day started as normal. And, as normal, I didn't want to get up. I was warm and comfortable in bed listening to the wind and the rain on the window. I was thinking that this must be the worst August in living memory. I heard Elizabeth coming up the stairs and so I curled up in a ball deep in bed and lay absolutely still, hoping she'd think I'd already got up. Or that I'd gone for an early morning run along the seafront. But she didn't fall for it.

She'd brought me a cup of tea, which was kind. I should have been more appreciative. I should have said, "Thank you, Elizabeth. What a wonderful sister you are. You are like a rainbow appearing after a storm. You are like the butterflies that swoop and flitter and play around the buttercups and daisies in a sun-drenched summer meadow." Instead, I just grunted and harrumphed as usual and used the poo word again.

In the kitchen, there was a fresh pot of tea brewing and Jaz was making toast. She seemed quite chirpy despite her culinary disaster of the night before. Sammi and Briony weren't up yet. There were more postcards from Mum and Dad. Both were well. Mum was looking forward to coming home. The picture on Mum's card was of a cactus in the desert. Dad's was a painting of sunflowers by Van Gogh. We propped them up against the marmalade jar, so the others would see them. It was reassuring to know that the sun was shining somewhere in the world.

Four days to go, and still tons to do. Could we finish it in time? Elizabeth and I cracked on with the painting and by midday we'd completed the largest wall. We stood back and surveyed the result.

"Mum will be amazed," Elizabeth said.

"I think it's pretty good," I agreed. "Maybe I'll be a mural painter. I bet there's a lot of money in that."

"What are we going to do about the floor?" Elizabeth asked.

The floor! I'd forgotten about that. "We'll just clean it up, shall we? Maybe give it a coat of varnish."

Briony wandered in, still wearing her black pyjamas and black dressing gown. "That wall looks cool."

"We're pleased with it," I said.

Briony yawned. "I'll get my camera. Have you seen the news yet?"

"Too busy working," I said. "Time and tide wait for no man."

"You're more right than you know," Briony said. "There have been unusually high tides all along this bit of coast. Floods everywhere."

"Oh no," Elizabeth said.

"Not here, thankfully," Briony said. "But there is storm damage. Cars blown off the roads, trees down. There are pictures on the net. Everywhere looks a mess."

"We haven't strayed into some time warp, have we?" I asked. "Maybe *we* think it's August, but it's really January."

At that point there was a loud wail in the doorway. There stood Sammi. Holding a rat by the tail. "Look!" She was sobbing. "It's Gerald. Kevin caught him."

No need to call the rat-catcher, then.

"Put it down," I said.

Sammi laid the rat carefully on the floor. Elizabeth gave Sammi a hug and took her into the kitchen to wash her hands. Briony and I looked at the body. "It doesn't look like one of Killer's usual victims,"

I said. "It still has its head on, for one thing."

Briony agreed. "But look, you can see teeth marks in the neck."

"Maybe Killer wasn't hungry," I said, "or just didn't fancy rat for breakfast."

"It's very wet, isn't it?"

I nodded. "Not surprising, in this weather. And what's that?" There was something green stuck to one of its legs. I bent down and picked it up. "How odd. It looks like seaweed. I didn't know rats swam in the sea."

"Perhaps it's a water rat," Briony said.

Elizabeth and Sammy came back.

"Poor Gerald," Sammi said. "We'll have to give him a proper burial."

"Look at this." I showed Elizabeth. "Looks like seaweed."

"I'm going to make him a special headstone," Sammi said, "for his grave. It'll say: *Gerald RIP.*"

"Where did you find him?" Briony asked.

"At the top of the cellar steps," Sammi said.

"The Gargoyle got him," I said.

We opened the door of the cellar and peered into the darkness. Elizabeth found the torch and shone it down. Its beam of light shimmered back at us.

Water everywhere. The cellar was flooded.

"I think Gerald must have drowned," Elizabeth said.

We peered some more. Briony went down to the bottom of the steps, to the water's edge.

"How deep is it?" I called down.

Briony dipped her bare toe in. "Five or six centimetres, I'd guess. Can you smell anything?" She dipped her finger into the inky water. Then she licked her finger.

"*Yeuch!!!*" Elizabeth said.

"It's salty," Briony called up. "The cellar's not only flooded – it's flooded with seawater."

"Wow," Sammi said. "We've got the seaside in our cellar!"

27
A Cellar Full
of Secrets

Wednesday – and only three days to go. Another card from Mum. This one had a picture of oranges on the front. The message said: *See you Saturday, love Mum.*

Yesterday afternoon Mrs Herring had given us a pile of tablecloths that she'd bought in a closing-down sale at the haberdasher's. None of them matched, so we'd decided to dye them dark blue. We didn't tell her about the flooded cellar. I was about to say something but Briony stopped me. Afterwards, Briony said that she didn't think Mrs Herring needed to know everything – just a feeling she had. I think Mrs Herring's fine, but I didn't argue. It's generally best not to argue with Briony – not unless you've a team of lawyers, professors and generally brainy people on your side to back up your arguments.

With Mrs Herring's help we finished the walls. There was still some touching-up to do, mind. It would probably take me another day to get it exactly as I wanted, but I wasn't sure there would be time.

I phoned the warehouse and they told me that the chairs would definitely be arriving in the afternoon, so we spent the morning moving the old café chairs out to the yard where we smashed them up for firewood. That was great fun. Then we had lunch. Jaz made us her speciality. You can probably guess what that was.

After lunch, Briony suggested we check out the cellar. The water had gone and she wanted to see if there was an obvious place where it could have come in, or if it had caused any damage. Jaz was working in the kitchen with Kavita and Sandy. Sammi was giving them a hand. She said she didn't want to come down into the cellar with us because the ghost lived there. Elizabeth was making a start on the café floor.

The cellar smelled terrible. Even worse than the time Dad's socks got trapped behind the heater for a month. It was a damp, rotten, fishy smell. And although the flood water had gone, the floor was still very wet and there were one or two puddles where the brick floor was uneven.

"With luck, the water's drowned the spiders," I said.

"But where could the water have come from?" Briony asked.

I shone my torch around and settled the beam

on something white. Briony picked it up. It was a tiny seashell.

"There must be a gap or hole or something," I said, shining the torch slowly around the walls. "If we find it, we could plug it up with some of Jaz's risotto."

The cellar was almost empty. In one corner was a stack of timber and some old screen-printing frames with no screens, covered in mildew. They were sodden. Leaning against one wall was an old printing press. It was a huge thing, rusty and mouldy. It would probably have been worth something, if it hadn't been in such bad repair. It looked like a table with great, thick legs and a metal top. And on the top was an iron press with a big handle, like a capstan.

There was no sign of a hole or gap in the brick wall. But the water must have come from somewhere. I balanced the torch on a lump of stone, to illuminate the cellar, and gingerly helped Briony move the wood and the frames, which fell apart in our hands. But there was nothing there.

"There could be a hole or something behind the press," Briony said. She shivered.

"What's up?" I asked.

"Nothing." She was whispering. "Just that feeling you get when someone walks over your grave."

"Don't be silly," I whispered back.

"To think that a murder happened here. Maybe it *is* haunted. Maybe Sammi's right."

I looked around. Was the troubled spirit of a murder victim still trapped in this dark, damp space? "I wonder if it was a man or woman who was killed," I said. "Or a child."

"I don't know. I've tried to find out but I can't find anything. No one seems to know anything about an ancient murder. There's nothing in the town records on the internet. Come on, let's try and move this press thing away from the wall."

I grabbed it and pulled, but it wouldn't budge. Then I tried pushing it from the side. It still wouldn't move.

"We have to both push at the same time," Briony said. "On the count of three."

Briony counted, and we both gave a huge shove. It moved about one centimetre. "We'll have to be more scientific," she said. "We need a lever."

Some of the timber we'd moved wasn't too bad. I found a thick plank unaffected by the damp and we wedged it behind the press.

"After three," Briony said again. "One, two, three . . . heave."

We gave it all we had. The press slid away from the wall, just a few centimetres. But it was definitely moving, sliding on the mud and sand on the floor.

"I think I can see something," Briony said. She picked up the torch and shone it behind the press. "Let's try again."

After several more goes, we'd moved the press quite a distance. And you could see a definite gap. The torchlight wasn't strong, but it looked as if the floor had sunk slightly, leaving a gap about three centimetres high and sixty centimetres long at the bottom of the wall.

"So," I said. "That's where the seawater comes in all right. But we're some way away from the sea. A couple of hundred metres, at least."

We thought about this for a bit. Then I felt something on my arm, like fingers lightly tapping me. It was a spider. A big one. I shrieked, and jumped so high, I nearly hit my head on the ceiling. The spider fell off me and stood still in a pool of pale torchlight, deciding whether or not to attack me, then scuttled away into the shadows.

"Spiders are harmless," Briony said. "Don't be a wimp."

"It took me by surprise, that's all."

"Are you thinking what I'm thinking?" Briony asked.

"About spiders?" I was thinking that maybe there was a huge nest of giant spiders living in the hole.

"No, no," she said. "I was thinking we could be near a storm drain or something. Or. . ." and she paused for effect, ". . . there could be a secret tunnel."

I thought about this for a few moments. It was entirely possible. "Remember what this place was called before it was Rubens' Rest?"

"Ah," said Briony, "of course. The Smugglers' Rest. It could be an old smugglers' tunnel. There are loads of smuggling stories told along this part of the coast. I bet there are lots of tunnels. Or were."

"Well, if it is a secret passage," I said, "how do we get into it?" I gave the wall a tentative push. Nothing happened. The bricks didn't look any different here from anywhere else. They were muddy and discoloured throughout the cellar.

"Wait!" Briony said. "I have a brilliant idea. Don't go away."

She left, leaving me standing in the dark.

"Wait!" I yelled.

I felt something on my foot. I hopped up and down, grabbed the torch and shone it at the floor.

Several large spiders were scuttling around.

There was a sudden noise. I jumped. I spun round. For a split second I thought of the ghost, the ghost I'd heard and that Sammi had seen.

Briony reappeared, out of breath. "Anything happen?"

There was a low whirring sound.

"Look out," I cried. The whole wall was vibrating. Small pieces of hard mortar and flakes of dried whitewash showered down from the ceiling, together with bits of crumbling brick and cobwebs.

Something was moving. You could clearly see the outline of a doorway in the wall now, about a metre high and sixty centimetres wide. And that section of the wall began to open and carried on opening, until it hit the press with a thud and could go no further.

We stood and stared. Transfixed.

"Wowee!" Briony said. "Look at that. A genuine smugglers' secret tunnel."

"What did you do?" I asked.

"Remember that switch that Thumbs found? In the PGR? The one that he said was live but didn't do anything? Well, now we know what it does."

We stared some more.

"Are we going to go in?" Briony asked.

"I don't know," I said. "Are we? It's probably full of spiders. The one that attacked me was huge. The size of a tennis ball."

"I think we should call the others."

"I agree. We should definitely get Elizabeth down here."

"I'll fetch her," Briony said.

"Wait!"

But Briony had disappeared again. It was all right for her. She *liked* spiders. After what seemed like an age, she reappeared with Elizabeth in tow. Elizabeth was as amazed as we were.

"We're going to have to go in," Briony said.

"What about the spiders?" I asked.

"They'll be gone by now," Briony said. "Anyway, they'll be more scared of you than you are of them."

"I'm not scared of them," I said.

Elizabeth laughed. "You'll be OK, then. Anyway, spiders don't like water."

"Let's see if we can move the press further out of the way," Briony said.

"What about water spiders?" I asked.

"I think you'll find they're called crabs," Elizabeth said.

"I don't like crabs either," I replied.

Moving the press sounded like a good plan. It took us a while and we were sweaty and wet and very muddy by the time we'd finished, but we managed to slide the giant contraption to one side, leaving a gap wide enough for the whole of the door section to open fully.

I shone the torch in. The tunnel was much bigger than you would have thought – high enough for a normal person to walk down, and quite wide. The wet floor was stone, the walls and arched ceiling were made of brick.

"Whoever built this made a good job of it," I said. "It must be a hundred years old."

"Probably older," Briony said. "Eighteenth century. Or before, even."

"Do you think the last owner knew about it?" Elizabeth asked.

"He must have done," I said. "He might even have had the electric switch put in. Even if he didn't, he'd have worked out what it was. Briony did. And he was an artist. That was probably his press blocking the doorway."

We stood in the torchlight and stared at the tunnel entrance.

Elizabeth shivered. "It's creepy."

"Are we going in?" Briony asked.

That was just what I was thinking. "Do you think it's safe? What if it were to cave in?"

"It should be all right," Briony said. "It's been there for hundreds of years. Why would it collapse now?"

"Well, I'm not going in," Elizabeth said. "The tunnel might collapse. Or we could get attacked by rats. Or . . . um . . . the tunnel could flood again. Or we could fall down a hole. . ."

"Or we could get attacked by giant spiders," I ventured. "All right, all right. If you're too scared to come, that's fine. Briony and I will go."

"I should stay here, too," Briony said. "I know how to operate the switch."

I couldn't believe that Briony was scared too. "Tricky, is it?" I enquired sarcastically. "One of those tricky switches that you have to move up and down?"

"No, but going into secret tunnels is a man's thing. It's written in the Rule Book. In the Secret Tunnel section."

"Are you suggesting that I go on my own?"

"Come on," Briony said. "You're a big, strong, brave man."

"I'm a small, weak boy!"

"There's absolutely nothing to be scared of," Briony

said. "Except for the spiders. But you're not scared of them, are you?"

I sighed theatrically. "OK, I'll go it alone. But I'll need the torch."

I climbed awkwardly through the doorway and stood up in the tunnel.

"Hello!" I said loudly. "Is anybody there?"

My voice bounced around the walls. And I'd be lying if I said I wasn't frightened. In theory, there was nothing to be scared of. Spiders are harmless, after all. And the tunnel had probably been there for two or three hundred years, so there was no real reason why it should collapse now. And rats? Well, if there were rats, they'd probably be more scared of me than me of them. They'd keep out of my way. Especially if they knew that my pet was Killer. And I didn't really believe in ghosts. Still . . . it was dark. And dank. And damp. And dismal. And dreary. And probably lots of other things beginning with D.

"What can you see?" Elizabeth whispered through the doorway.

"Nothing yet," I said. I walked forward slowly, very slowly, being careful not to slip on the muddy, sandy stone floor, shining the torch ahead of me, keeping a look-out for spiders. It might have been my imagination, but I was sure I could hear the sea. The tunnel turned a corner and I cautiously made my way forward, aware that I'd lost sight of the doorway.

The tunnel opened into a small room. There was something propped up against the wall.

My heart leapt to my throat. I stood still, frozen.

I wasn't prepared for this.

28
To Tell or
Not to Tell

The skeleton was sitting propped up against the wall. I felt a bit dizzy, so I took a few deep breaths to calm myself down. After all, it was only a skeleton. It couldn't hurt me. I could feel my heart thudding in my chest.

"Wilf! Wilf!"

Elizabeth was calling me.

"Wilf! Are you all right?"

"It's OK," I managed to call back. "I've found something. . ."

"What is it?"

"You'll never guess." I moved slowly forward towards the bones. If the person had been wearing clothes, they were now long gone. Rotted away, no doubt, and washed away. I shone my torch around the room. The walls were brick and covered in green slime. The floor was wet, sandy and muddy. There was a pile of what looked like driftwood against one wall, maybe the remains of barrels. Perhaps this had once been a storeroom used by smugglers. Set in the end wall was a big wooden door with two heavy, rusty bolts drawn across it.

I turned back to the skeleton. It seemed to be well preserved. There was no obvious sign of foul play, as they say on television detective shows. No knife sticking out of the ribs or anything like that. I stood staring at it, wondering what to do.

"Wilf! Wilf!" It was Elizabeth again. "What's going on?"

"I'm coming," I said. And I made my way back to the cellar.

"Are you OK?" Briony asked me. "You look like you've seen a ghost."

"You didn't see a ghost, did you?" Elizabeth asked.

"No," I said. "What I saw was very real."

"What was it?"

"A skeleton."

Elizabeth shrieked.

"You're joking," Briony said.

"Take a look for yourselves."

"You *are* joking," Elizabeth said.

"I'm not. Honest! Like I say, go and have a look."

"In there?" Elizabeth said. "In the tunnel?"

"Yeah. There's a room just round the corner.

Go on. It's only a skeleton. It won't hurt you."

Briony looked at Elizabeth and Elizabeth looked at Briony.

"What do you think?" Briony asked. "I think we should."

"It looks like a bit of a squeeze. . ."

It took a while for my sisters to gather up the courage, but at last they decided to take a look. I stayed on guard while they climbed through the doorway. I listened to their loud, nervous chattering as they made their way into the room. The cellar was dark with them gone and only the light from the cellar door above spilling down the steps.

There was a muffled shriek.

"You OK?" I called through the hole.

"Oh my!" Briony called back. "It's amazing."

I could hear Elizabeth urging Briony to go back. Briony wanted to stay and examine the skeleton. I'd guessed it wouldn't be long before Briony's scientific curiosity took over. But after a few minutes they both reappeared.

"Let's go back up," Elizabeth said. "I feel queasy."

"Maybe we should close the door and move the press back against the wall," I said.

"Why?" Elizabeth asked. "The police will only

have to move it again."

"I'm not sure we should call the police," I said.

Elizabeth stared at me. "What? We find a dead body and you say we shouldn't call the police. What are you talking about?"

Surprisingly, Briony came to my aid. "Wilf's right," she said. "Maybe we shouldn't tell the police yet,"

"Why not?"

"Let's just close the door and move the press back, and I'll explain," I said.

So Briony went back upstairs and operated the switch. And without too much trouble we slid the press back into place. Then a visit to the bathroom to clean up, before we met in my bedroom.

"Reasons for not telling the police," I said. I'd given this a bit more thought while I was having a shower. It was my first shower since Mum and Dad had gone, but I probably needed one. I had the stink of the cellar all over me. I have to say, I quite enjoyed it – the shower, not the stink. I can see why some people shower as often as they do. But I don't think I'll be making a habit of it.

"Reason one. We'll have police everywhere. You know what those crime scenes look like on the telly. It will seriously get in the way of the grand opening."

"But won't we be in trouble?" Elizabeth asked. "Concealing a crime or something? I'm sure we'll be breaking the law."

"Reason number two. There is no way we can do anything until Mum gets back. We can't call the police. If we speak to them, they'll want to talk to Mum and Dad, won't they? And then what do we do? Mum and Dad will be in trouble for deserting us. We can't pretend it was all arranged and that someone is looking after us. We don't even know exactly where Mum is – we don't have her friend's address. We really, really have to wait for her to come home."

"That's a good point," Elizabeth said. "I hadn't thought about it properly. We can't get Mum and Dad into trouble, can we?"

"Anyway," I said. "It's not a dead body. You saw it. It's an old skeleton. It's probably a smuggler and it's probably been there for centuries. It could even be the murder victim from hundreds of years ago. Whatever it is, a few more days isn't going to make any difference, is it?"

"If it's really old," Elizabeth said, "Time Team might

want to see it and we'll be on the telly."

"But what if. . ." Briony said, and she put her hand to her mouth. "Oh no. . ."

"What?" Elizabeth asked.

"The skeleton," Briony said. "What if it's John Montague?"

Elizabeth gasped, and there was a long silence while we digested the information.

"It couldn't be, could it?" Elizabeth asked.

"Why not?" Briony said. "He went missing. Nobody knows what happened to him. Now we've found a skeleton in a secret passage in his house."

"Briony's right," I said. "It could be him. Oh dear. . ."

"But we still can't call the police, even if it is him. We can't get Mum and Dad into trouble," Elizabeth said.

I stood up and peered out of the window, thinking. We hadn't tried very hard to find Mum or Dad, once we'd realised they'd both gone. Mum and Dad might understand. They knew that the five of us could cope on our own. But I didn't think the police would be very impressed.

The sky was slate grey and it was still blowing half a gale. I looked at my sisters sitting anxiously on my bed.

"It might not be John Montague, anyway," Elizabeth said at last.

"But if it is," Briony said, "how did he get there? Did he go into the tunnel and then get trapped?"

"Could be," I said. "We know how bad the wiring is. That doorway's worked by some kind of electric motor. If there was a power cut or something. . ."

"But there's another possibility," Briony said. "Supposing he was in there and someone pushed the press in front of the door so that it wouldn't open? There might have been a murder in the cellar hundreds of years ago – but maybe there was another one five years ago, too."

That would be very bad news, I thought. A murder investigation. We certainly wouldn't be able to open the café then. There would be police officers everywhere. And reporters.

"Let's just think about it," I said, "before we do anything."

"We could tell Mrs Herring," Elizabeth said. "She'd know what to do."

"Definitely don't tell her," Briony said. "I'm not sure I trust her. And don't tell Sammi and Jaz. Not yet. If we tell Jaz, the news will be all over town in no time. You know what she's like."

"She can keep a secret," Elizabeth said. "She hasn't told anyone about the mole on my bottom, has she?"

We both gave our sister one of those long silent looks that says – she has, you know. The whole world knows about the mole on your bottom.

"And we don't want to upset Sammi," I said. "She'll get scared about the ghost again. Mum needs to be here when Sammi finds out."

The bedroom door swung open, making us jump. It was Sammi.

"What are you all doing up here? I've been looking for you everywhere. We've got a visitor. He wanted to speak to Mum but I said she wasn't in. So he said could he talk to you. I think he wants to inspect us."

"Who is it?" I asked.

"He says he's an inspector."

29
More Ghosts

"Good afternoon, children," said Inspector Carpet.

He was standing near the window, sipping a cup of tea. His coat was piled on a table, which reminded me that we needed a coat stand for customers' coats. He smiled. "Nice cuppa, this. Your sister served me, and very well, too, if I may say so, considering her lack in the years department. Yes, a very nice cup of tea, and not too much milk." He took another sip and put the cup carefully back on to its saucer. "Very nice."

"Hello again," Elizabeth said. "Well, what can we do for you?"

"Would I be right in assuming that your mum's not in, then?"

"You would be," I said. "She's at her origami class."

"Martial arts, eh?" The inspector nodded sagely. "I used to do a bit of that when I was younger. I'm a bit stiff these days, though, due to the arthritis. It comes to us all. One minute you're apprehending villains and the next, it's all you can do to get out of bed in the morning."

"So," I said, "what can we do for you?"

"She's a busy woman, your mum, isn't she? What with the abseiling and the karate. What happened to the chairs?"

"We have some new ones coming," Elizabeth said. "They should be arriving any moment."

"That's good. You'll need chairs. I don't mind telling you that I'm not a fan of restaurants where you have to stand up all the time. They're a bit too modern for me."

"You prefer the sitting down type?" I asked.

He nodded. "This is a very nice card."

I realised with horror that he was holding the most recent postcard from Mum in his hand. Oh no! What had she written on it? I tried to remember.

"Ah . . . Spain," he said slowly, "The trouble is, I can't eat oranges. They give me a migraine."

He turned the card over. Elizabeth was staring at him with her mouth open. I nudged her with my foot and gave her a meaningful look.

"I took my wife to Spain once. We didn't go to the usual tourist places. Lovely people, the Spanish – very gentle."

"I don't think they are," Elizabeth said. "What about bull fights?"

"No, no, no. . ." the inspector said, and chuckled. "You mustn't believe all you read, young lady. The bulls don't get hurt. In fact, they really enjoy it."

"I don't think so," Briony said. "Last year hundreds of bulls died in bull fights. It's a cruel and barbaric sport."

The inspector smiled and turned the card over. "This is a strange message. *See you Saturday. Love Mum.*"

"It's from Dad," I said, "saying he loves Mum. Er . . . he's been working away from home. Did we say? Anyway . . . um . . . he's coming back for the grand opening of the café on Saturday."

The inspector pulled a small notebook from his pocket and flipped it open. "It says here that he's working in France."

"That's right," Briony added. "He was. But he moved to Spain. And um . . . well, we shouldn't say, really, but he and Mum fell out."

"Yes," I said. "He didn't want her to go abseiling any more in case she got hurt."

"But he wants to make up," Briony said. "So he wrote *Love Mum* on the card."

We paused for breath. You could almost see the inspector's mind working, like a bus trying to reverse into the parking space left by a Renault Clio.

"Makes perfect sense," he said. "So, you're opening on Saturday."

"That's right," Elizabeth said. "And you are invited."

"Why, thank you."

"And bring your wife," Elizabeth said.

"Oh, I won't be able to do that. She's . . . well, she's . . . er . . . gone now." He swallowed, and rubbed the corner of his eye with his thumb.

"I'm sorry," Elizabeth said. "Did she . . . you know. . ."

"Die?" Briony added. "Is she dead?" The inspector sniffed. "Not exactly. . ."

"Badly wounded?" I ventured.

He shook his head. "No. She ran away with a chef from Cocklesfield. He was a really nice chap, actually."

"Well, we must be getting on," I said.

"We used to go to his restaurant. You know, before . . . before he and . . . um . . . well, he used to do a lovely lasagne. Did you give your mum my message?"

I tried to think what he meant.

"About Neighbourhood Watch?" Elizabeth said. "Yes, we did. She said she was very interested, but could you see her about it after the opening. She's very busy at the moment, as you can imagine."

Elizabeth is not usually brilliant at thinking on her feet, but I was proud of her on this occasion. The inspector was writing in his little book.

"There we are," he said. "And I've made a note of the opening, too. I'll certainly pop along."

The inspector waved his hand in the general direction of the walls. "The decorating . . . not bad. I do a little bit of decorating, you know, mainly for friends. I do like to keep busy. And you've certainly made a good job of the painting. You're a talented young man."

"Thank you," I said.

"Mind you, I still think a nice Mediterranean scene would be better, with a blue sea and palm trees. The chap who owned this place before you was an artist, you know."

"We did know, actually," I said.

"He was very good. I wonder what did happen to him," the inpsector said. "Ah, well, I expect he'll turn up again one day, you know, revisiting his old haunts."

There was an awful silence.

"Anyway," Elizabeth said, after what seemed about half an hour, "I expect you must go. I bet you've got lots to do."

And at last we managed to usher Inspector Carpet out of the door.

"I could do with a cuppa myself," Elizabeth said.

Vampyre sensed that the end was near. Soon it would be reunited with its beloved master. A shaft of moonlit fell through the gaping hole in the roof on to its scaled head. Soon, so soon, it thought, as it ripped the trap-door from its hinge and threw it aside. It clambered down on to the landing and looked around. It spied the door. Should it investigate the human, or make its way down the stairs to where the Gargoyle was chained? A key! The human would have a key. It moved slowly towards the door . . . my door! So, so soon . . . It lifted its head and cried to its master, "I will be there soon. Waaaaaaaaaaaaaaaaiiiiiiiiiiiiiiiiiiiyyyyyyyyyyyyyyyyyyyyy. . ."

I woke up.

A police siren echoed through the night and faded away. The wind had died down. Everything was quiet. I looked at the clock. Two in the morning. I listened hard, half-expecting to hear the ghost again. But there was nothing.

I thought about the amazing day we'd had. Were we doing the right thing, not telling the police? I was sure a few more days weren't going to hurt, no matter what the circumstances of the victim's death. If the skeleton was John Montague, then the really worrying thing was *how* he'd died. If he'd simply become trapped – well, that wasn't too bad. Probably it was his own fault. But what if he *had* been murdered? If he'd been killed, then the murderer could still be around. But the killer wouldn't be interested in us, would he? So why should we worry? But it *was* a worry – the thought of a murderer coming into the café.

These thoughts started whizzing around my head and I couldn't seem to stop them. I don't know about you, but when I'm in bed, in the middle of the night, things seem to grow out of all proportion. I started wondering what would happen if the murderer discovered we had found the body. He would have to shut us up so that we didn't tell the police. I imagined him killing us and dragging our bodies through the secret passageway and into that tiny room, blocking up the door with the old printing press. And I imagined spiders running over our dead bodies. And crabs nibbling at our dead toes. I think I dozed off just as the giant lobsters arrived.

I woke up again to hear talking coming from downstairs. It was still dark. The clock said three o'clock. I grabbed my dressing-gown and went down to investigate. Everyone was in Sammi's room.

Jaz was sitting next to her little sister on the bed, her arm around her.

"Sammi thought she heard the ghost again."

"It was horrid," Sammi said. "I don't like this house. I want to go home. I want Mummy back."

"There, there," Jaz said. "Mum will be back on Saturday. That's only three days. Two days, really. Two more sleeps and Mum will be back from her holiday."

"Well, I want to move," Sammi said. "I don't like this house. It's haunted."

"No it's not," Briony said. "There's no such thing as ghosts, Sammi. Really, truly."

"It was Gerald's ghost," Sammi said.

"Rats don't have ghosts," I said.

"Yes they do. I heard it. It was coming from downstairs. It was coming from the cellar."

Back in bed once more, as I drifted off to sleep, I could see

197

the press in the cellar. It was moving all on its own. No – something was pushing it. The secret door was opening, pushing the press out of the way, gradually pushing the press away from the wall. It was the Gargoyle. It was back, it was free, and it had a score to settle. It squeezed through the narrow gap and into the cellar. It was sniffing the dark, damp cellar air. Picking up my scent. And making its way up the cellar steps to find me.

I sat up. My heart was thumping.

I clambered out of bed, put my dressing-gown on again and grabbed my duvet. Maybe Elizabeth wouldn't mind me sleeping on the floor of her room. She might like a bit of reassurance – someone to remind her that ghosts don't exist.

30
The Name over
the Shop

By the time I woke, it was light and Elizabeth was up
and doing. I climbed into her empty bed. I'd not had
the most comfortable night. Maybe I could sneak some
extra sleep before Elizabeth came to get me up.

Two days to go and my head was full of so many
things I still had to do. First, I was missing our
parents. Sammi goes on about missing Mum all the
time. Jaz and Elizabeth talk about her a lot as well.
Me? Well, I was missing Dad, too. I know he's pretty
hopeless, but he is fun! Briony hasn't said much on the
subject – she keeps her feelings well hidden. But I'm
sure she misses them too. A couple of days ago I caught
her talking to the dummy in the dining-room. But
I didn't say anything. I didn't want to embarrass her.

Secondly, there was the secret passage and the
skeleton. A possible murder and the killer still on the
loose? No – if it was John Montague, then the killer
would be long gone. He wouldn't hang around. And
anyway, it was probably the skeleton of a smuggler

and we were getting all worried for nothing. I thought it was unlikely to be connected to the ancient murder.

Thirdly, there was the matter of the ghost. Briony says it doesn't exist. But I think she's wrong. A haunted house is one thing, but if it's keeping us all awake, especially poor old Sammi, then something has to be done about it. Maybe we should get the local priest along to exorcise it. I wonder how they exorcise ghosts. Does the priest walk them up and down the corridors on a lead, like a dog? (Just joking.)

And, fourthly, how on earth were we going to be ready to open on time? Only two days to go, and still loads to do. The food, the floors, the chairs, the music. . . At least the walls were finished. I was really pleased with the result. I hoped Mum and Dad would like it. I don't expect it was what they'd planned, but then, I don't think they'd really planned anything much.

I could hear a tapping sound. I lay in the dark of the bed and listened. *Tap, tap, tap.* It seemed to be something, or someone, banging on the window. I peered over the top of the duvet. A baby seagull was peering back at me through the grimy glass. Did it want to come in?

I pulled myself out of bed and went across the

room. The seagull was perched on the narrow window ledge. Elizabeth's room, like mine, is on the top floor and there is quite a drop down to the street below. The bird was so close, I could touch it. Well, I could have touched it, if the glass hadn't been in the way. The bird was staring at me. It was still in its puffy brown plumage and I wondered if it could fly. I scanned the sky for some sign of its mother.

I began to slide the window up. I had some daft notion of catching it and taking it somewhere safe. But it obviously didn't like that idea and jumped, then half-flew and half-flapped down to the street. I worried that it might get run over, but there was no traffic and it would probably be OK.

Time to get dressed. Lots to do. I wondered if I should have another shower but decided against it. Once a month was quite enough.

Then I remembered Killer. What if the cat found the baby bird wandering about? It would be cat food. I rushed downstairs to Sammi's room. She was still fast asleep and Killer was sitting on the bottom of her bed, dribbling and chewing the corner of her duvet. He gave me a friendly snarl. I breathed a sigh of relief.

Downstairs, I found Elizabeth and Briony in the café washing tables. I told them about the seagull and we went out to look for it, but it had gone,

"The mother bird probably found it," Briony said.

"There's a fresh pot of tea," Elizabeth said. "And the tablecloths are in the washing machine."

"Good old Mrs Herring," I said.

"But I'm getting a bit worried. We're not going to be ready in time, are we? And where are the chairs?" Elizabeth asked.

I rang the warehouse and they were very apologetic. They promised me faithfully that they would deliver today. The chairs had been loaded into the van – but yesterday the driver had been taken ill and hadn't been able to deliver them. He'd eaten some dodgy prawns, apparently. And so their reserve driver had come back early from his holiday in Dudley, just so that they could get the chairs to us on time. I thought that was jolly good service.

Today I was going to paint the name over the café. Thumbs was supplying a ladder.

As he carried the ladder over the road he failed to notice the approaching cyclist, an elderly gentleman in a tweed suit. Fortunately the man wasn't too badly hurt. We managed to placate him by offering him a free meal at the grand opening.

Eventually we got the ladder up and Thumbs held

it while I did the painting. It took two goes. First I had to paint a dark blue background, which I left to dry for a couple of hours. Next, I painted on the letters. By the time I'd finished, a little crowd had gathered to applaud my efforts.

Seeing the name over the shop was fantastic: *The Comic Café* – in cheery red and yellow. I felt a real sense of achievement – not a pretend one but a real one. Very much like the way Saint Rublev must have felt after painting a particularly tricky portrait of the Virgin Mary. Briony took my photo for the scrapbook as I stood proudly in the café doorway, paintbrush in hand.

It was that evening that I made a startling discovery – something that had been niggling me for some time. So I called Briony and Elizabeth up to my room. Sammi and Jaz were downstairs watching *I'm a Celebrity – Throw me a Peanut*, where comedians and soap stars live in a zoo in place of the animals. It was mildly amusing watching them swinging on bars in the monkey cages.

"Exhibit One," I said, and I showed them the Red

Square painting. "A painting by John Montague."

"Not very good, is it?" Elizabeth said. "I reckon a two-year-old child could do that."

"I don't know," Briony said, "I think it's probably quite accomplished."

"Nice word," I said. "And Exhibit Two." I handed them the postcard I'd bought at the art gallery.

Briony caught on immediately. "The postcard is a reverse photo of the picture here."

"That's right," I said.

"Hang on a minute," Elizabeth said. "Let me see . . . you showed us this postcard before. . ."

"Yes."

"And you said it was a reverse image of the picture in the gallery. You thought it was funny that the person who took the photo had printed it back to front for the postcard."

"That's right. You can tell it's wrong because the square is on a slight slant. You have to look carefully, mind."

"And now you're saying," Briony went on, "that the painting by Montague is also a reverse of the postcard – but the same way round as the original?"

"Yes, I said.

"Well, there's nothing odd about that," Elizabeth said. "He copied the original. It looks like the original.

So what?"

"Exhibit Three," I said. And I held up a photographic slide. "Look at this." Elizabeth and Briony took turns to hold it up to the window. "I found this still in the slide projector in the shed."

"I still don't get it," Elizabeth said.

Briony frowned. "I think I do. The slide is also the wrong way round."

"You've got it!" I yelled.

"It's a mirror image of the painting. And so is the postcard," Briony said.

"Yes," I went on. "So what are the chances of the photo for the slide and the photo for the postcard both being wrong? Pretty slim, wouldn't you say?"

"But so what?" Elizabeth said again. "What are you both going on about?"

"Well, dear sister," Briony said. "What Wilf is saying, is – maybe the postcard and the slide are *not* back to front, but the right way round. Which means the painting in the gallery and this one by John Montague are the ones that are the wrong way round."

"But that's impossible," Elizabeth said.

"No," Briony said, "not if they really are of the original – and the painting in the gallery is a fake! A forgery."

I looked at the postcard again, as I tried to get my thoughts in some kind of order.

"OK," I said at last. "How about this. John Montague paints copies of well-known pictures. He uses a slide projector to throw the image on to the canvas. That way, as he fills it in with line and colour, it is exactly true to the original. It's a well-known technique. But he puts the slide into the projector the wrong way round. So the image is back to front. And the painting he paints is back to front."

"And. . ." Briony adds, "he substitutes his forgery for the one in the gallery. The painting you found in the shed was a practice one."

"Well, I was thinking that," I said. "But how could the painting in the gallery be a fake – painted by John Montague?"

"Aha – well," Briony said. "Something else I found out. As well as working for the gallery, John Montague was a trustee. He used to advise them on acquisitions."

"Oh my," I gasped.

"This is scary," Briony said.

"Very scary," I agreed. "As a trustee he would have been, well, trusted. . ."

"Exactly."

Elizabeth was staring at us as though we were crazy. "What's scary? What are you going on about?"

"It's like this," Briony told Elizabeth. "Supposing John Montague copied the Red Square painting, and then substituted it for the real one. In other words, stole the real one."

"Yes," I said. "Imagine that. John Montague – a forger – and a thief! I wonder what happened to the original painting?"

"I expect he sold it for loads of money," Elizabeth said.

"Wow!" Briony exclaimed. "I've thought of something else. If the skeleton in the cellar is John Montague. . ."

"What?" Elizabeth asked.

"Well," Briony said. "What if his murder had something to do with the painting? Or what if he was killed before he sold it? Then the painting could still be here in the house."

"Oh, don't be silly. Someone would have found it by now," Elizabeth said.

"Maybe," I said. "But it could be hidden somewhere – somewhere in the house. I know it's unlikely . . . but just think – a painting worth thousands of pounds. . ."

"I do hope we're wrong," Briony said. "Because if that *is* the body of John Montague and his death is somehow related to the theft of the painting. . ."

"Then the murderer would have taken the painting," Elizabeth said.

"Unless he was murdered because he wouldn't tell his killer where he had hidden it. . ." Briony just wouldn't give up. And I thought she had a point.

"Then his killer could still be around," I said.

We all stared at one another.

"No, no," Briony said, "we're imagining all this. The picture in the gallery must be the real one. There was *no* theft. The body *isn't* John Montague. And we're getting ourselves worked up over nothing."

"That's right," I said. "Nothing to worry about at all."

"Exhibit One." Elizabeth pointed at the painting. "Could that be the original? The real one?"

I shook my head. "Definitely not. It's the wrong way round. And look, he smudged it. He left it to rot in the shed. No, this a trial version. This isn't the real one."

"If it's a trial version," Briony said, "what about the other two pictures you found in the shed? Are they trial versions too? Could there be *three* forgeries hanging in the gallery?"

31
The Calm before
the Storm

I woke up. My bedroom was full of smoke. I grabbed my dressing-gown, but it was wrapped around the hook on the door and wouldn't come free. Naked, I ran on to the landing. Which way to go? I could see flames and, silhouetted against the flames, the black, bat-like shape of Vampyre rushing towards me. I ran down the stairs but the stairs began to rock and shake. And there below me was the Gargoyle, waiting. Its slimy arms were reaching out for me. The stairs collapsed as the flames took hold and I fell towards it. Falling, falling. . .

I woke up.

I could smell smoke.

I grabbed my dressing-gown and rushed downstairs. Everyone was in the kitchen and Jaz was looking glum. A cloud of black smoke hung in the air like a giant depressed thought-bubble.

"It was an experiment that went wrong," Elizabeth explained.

On the table lay a pile of very black burnt biscuits.

"Kryptonite Krackers," Jaz said. "I think I've overcooked them a bit."

Friday. One day to go and still a hundred things to do. But the end was in sight. If the café could talk, it would be saying, "Come in, admire my newly-dyed blue tablecloths, admire my freshly-painted walls, thrill to Superman, Spiderman and the X-Men, read my marvellous menus, order my fantastic food."

But it wouldn't be saying, "Sit at my tables" – because the chairs still hadn't arrived. I phoned the warehouse and the manager explained that the van had set out on time, but a cow had wandered into its path and the replacement driver had swerved and driven into a telephone box. The van was fine, but the collision had broken the windows in the telephone box and there was glass everywhere, and the van had got a puncture. And for some reason the spare wheel was back at the warehouse. But not to worry, because the puncture had been repaired and the chairs would be with us within the hour. In fact, the warehouse manager was so upset that he had promised that if anything else went wrong with the van, he would personally carry the chairs round to us one at a time to make sure we had them for the opening. Well, you can't say fairer than that, can you?

I suppose I should have been pleased that everything was coming together and that we might open on time. But I still had the floor to sort out. Everywhere was a mess and you could smell burnt biscuit all over the house. On top of that, I kept thinking about the skeleton in the secret room and the fake paintings in the art gallery. We'd have to tell someone and have the paintings checked – that is, if anyone believed our theory. I'm not sure I believed it myself, to be honest.

On the plus side, the last big Tesco order arrived bang on time. Jaz and her friends were busy in the kitchen getting things organised. Every now and then they would burst into a chorus of "Food, Glorious Food!" We did a production of *Oliver* at my last school and it was great fun. I was one of Fagin's gang. My job was to pick pockets. I considered myself one of the family.

Mum rang, and we all talked to her. It was brilliant to hear her voice. My sisters were all crying. Even Briony. We'd agreed that if she did ring, we wouldn't tell her about Dad. She'd only panic, and she was coming home tomorrow so there seemed no point. Sammi nearly let it slip about opening the café, but Elizabeth grabbed the phone from her just in time. Mum said the plane would be landing early in the morning. We should expect her home at midday. Perfect.

Jaz and her mates were in the kitchen and the rest of us were having a mid-morning break, standing round one of the tables drinking Cokes and sharing a Kit Kat, when Killer, who had been snoozing on the counter, suddenly leapt up and growled.

The door opened and Mrs Herring came in.

"Maybe sun vill be out tomorrow," she said, shaking the rain from her umbrella.

"It will be a glorious sunny day," I said.

"Because Mum's coming home," Sammi added.

"I'm looking forward to meeting her," Mrs Herring said.

Mrs Herring had agreed to be a waitress. "I've got black outfit that will be ideal," she said, "and vite pinny."

"Just the job," I said.

"Vat is zat funny smell?"

"That would be the Kryptonite Krackers," I said. "One of Jaz's experiments went a bit wrong. The smell doesn't want to go away."

"Ah, never mind. So . . . everyzing is ready?" Mrs Herring asked.

"Apart from the chairs," I said. "Who'd have thought it? Rubens' Rest transformed into the Comic Café in, what . . . two weeks?"

"You've done vell," Mrs Herring said. "And comic book heroes are definite improvement on nudes."

"I thought you liked Rubens," I said.

"No, not really. I don't know much about art. I know vat I like, zough. And it isn't big fat bottoms."

"But they were well painted," I went on. "John Montague was a good artist."

"I suppose he vas," Mrs Herring said. "I didn't know him very vell." She glanced at her watch. "I must go. Now . . . vhere did I put handbag?" She hunted around. "I'm sure I put it down here."

We all started looking.

"I've got an idea," Briony said and disappeared into the PGR.

After a couple of minutes she reappeared. "Is this it?"

"Da!" Mrs Herring said. "Vhere vas it?"

"Killer," Briony said with a sheepish look. "I think he . . . er . . . borrowed it."

"Zat bloody cat!" Mrs Herring inspected the bag

for damage and teeth marks. "Vell . . . it seems OK."

"Sorry," I said.

Mrs Herring sighed. "Don't vorry about it." She opened the door, peered up at the grey, rainy sky and put up her umbrella. "I'll see you tomorrow, zen."

"Another cup of tea, anyone?" Elizabeth asked.

"That was interesting," Briony said.

"What was?" Elizabeth asked.

"Oh, I'll tell you later. We've got another visitor."

It was Ironhead. He slipped off his raincoat and deposited it in a heap by the door. "Never seen so much rain. No point busking today. Everywhere's deserted. Just stopped by to wish you good luck."

"Thanks," Elizabeth replied.

"It *is* tomorrow, isn't it?"

"No," I said. "It's today all day today."

"What?" Ironhead looked confused.

"I'm going to make another pot of tea," Elizabeth said, "Would you like a cup?"

"Just what the doctor ordered," Ironhead said. "So – you've painted the front."

"That's right," I said.

"Nice name. The Comic Café. I like it."

"Thanks."

"What happened to the chairs?"

"We've bought some new ones. They'll be here later," I said.

"Good. Chairs are very useful in a café. Did you play my CD?"

"I did," I said. "Very enjoyable. Especially the track 'Killer Rats Gnawed Off My Leg'."

"Oh," Sammi cried softly.

"Really?" Ironhead grinned. "You liked that? That was one of mine. The others didn't want to include it on the album."

"Why was that?"

"They said it was too violent."

"I am surprised," I said.

"Poor Gerald." Sammi threw her arms around Elizabeth. "Why did he have to die?"

Ironhead looked confused again.

"Don't worry," I said. "Gerald was just someone Sammi knew once."

"What happened to your band, then?" Elizabeth asked.

"We split up. There were musical differences. I wanted to play heavier stuff."

"Heavier?" I said. "Heavier than 'The Meteorite That Obliterated Planet Earth'?"

"That was one of mine, too. Well, the others just

wanted to be a pop band. Have number one hits, become rich and famous – you know. . ."

"And you didn't?" I asked.

"Not by playing rubbish," he said. "It's a question of integrity. Also, the singer had a nasty accident. We had er . . . a disagreement and that led to a fight and he . . . um . . . accidentally fell off the stage during a sound check."

"Oh dear," Elizabeth said.

"Then I accidentally dropped a monitor cab on top of him."

"What's a monitor cab?" Elizabeth asked.

"Well, it's a big wooden box with speakers in. So that the band can hear the vocals."

"And it's heavy, is it?"

Ironhead nodded. "You could say that."

Elizabeth and I looked at one another, neither of us sure what to say.

"I was a bit violent in them days. It was an accident, though. I'm not violent now. I've changed my ways."

"Are you coming to the grand opening tomorrow?" Elizabeth asked him.

"Yeah. What time?"

"Eleven o'clock," I said. "There's a free cup of tea and a Batman bun for the first ten customers."

"Ah yes, I saw that on the posters."

"Briony did the posters," Elizabeth said. Briony gave a little pleased-with-herself grin.

"Will your mum be here?" Ironhead enquired.

"Oh yes," Elizabeth said. "Of course."

"She's not here now, though."

"No," I said. "She's having her eyebrows dyed."

"Nice. Can you smell anything?"

"No," I said.

"There's a peculiar smell. Smells like burning."

"That would be the Kryptonite," I said.

"It smells more like burnt biscuits. Er . . . I was wondering . . . would you like me to bring my saxophone along?"

I caught the sideways look that Elizabeth threw at me. It said – No, no, no . . . please don't let him play his saxophone at the opening. I tossed the look back. She caught it.

Then I had a brilliant idea. "Do you still play guitar?"

"Yeah, I strum a bit."

"Well, it's just that the saxophone would probably be a bit loud in here, don't you think? But guitar – that would be nice."

I had a sudden image of Ironhead playing deafening

Aerosmith riffs on an electric guitar plugged into a giant amplifier with piles of monitor cabs. "It *is* an acoustic guitar?"

"Yeah. I've got an acoustic. Great idea. I'll go home now and practise. Get some tunes together."

We watched him go. Outside, he passed our next visitor, Frank Meek. We could see them through the window. They exchanged a greeting, shook hands and had a brief chat.

"You see that?" Elizabeth remarked. "They know one another. Who'd have thought that?"

"That's interesting," Briony said. "Very interesting."

Frank came in. I was pleased to see he didn't have Prints with him.

"Hi, kids," he said. "Your mum in?"

"Hello, Frank," Elizabeth said.

"The gang's all here, eh?"

"Mum's out right now," Elizabeth said.

"I never seem to find her in, do I?" Frank said. "I thought maybe today – third time lucky."

"We're not looking for a car," I said.

"You never know," he said. "Nice tablecloths! I have to say, you've made a fantastic job of this place. I like the way you've painted the front, too. *You* did that, then?"

I nodded.

"I think John would have approved," he said. "He had an eye for colour. He loved the Jag I found him. It was mulberry red. If he were here now, eh?"

An image of the skeleton propped up in the dark passageway floated into my mind and I found myself thinking of the skeleton driving a car. I tried to divert it up a quiet side road. . .

"Are you coming to the grand opening?" Elizabeth asked.

"Most certainly. Wouldn't miss it for the world. What about your dad?"

"He won't be able to make it," I said. "He's working abroad."

"Shame," Frank said. "He should be here, helping to get the café up and running."

"Someone's got to pay for the work," I said.

"It's Mum's project really," Elizabeth said.

"Where are the chairs, then?"

"We've bought some new ones. They'll be here later," I said.

"You should have asked me," Frank said. "I could have got you some at trade price. Well, must be off. Time is money. . . Funny smell. Can you smell anything – or is it just me?"

"I think it's you," I said.

"But it's not Mum's project, is it?" I said to Elizabeth when he'd gone.

Elizabeth shrugged. "I'm getting fed up with people asking us where Mum and Dad are, aren't you?"

"Mum'll be home tomorrow," I said. "So we won't have to put up with it any more."

"Hooray!" Sammi said.

"That will be a relief," Elizabeth said.

"Do you know," I said, "that's the third time Frank's been to see us. Surely he doesn't want to sell us a car *that* desperately."

"It is odd," Briony said. "It's odd that he knows Ironhead, too."

"Why is that odd?" Elizabeth asked. "I expect everyone in the town knows Ironhead. When he's playing the saxophone, it's hard to ignore him."

"I've been doing some serious thinking," Briony said.

"And?"

"Well, I've been putting two and two together."

"And what does it make?" Sammi asked.

"I'll tell you all when I've worked it out properly." Briony stood up and produced her camera. "Smile!" We obliged. "Meanwhile, I'm going to make a collage of all the photos I've taken. It will document the change from derelict slum to beautifully presented eating establishment. I'll frame it."

"Excellent," I said. "It could go in the window."

"One day left," Sammi said. "Hooray!"

Elizabeth gave her a hug. "Yes, only one day. You've been very patient. I'll tell Mum what a good girl you've been."

Killer appeared in the doorway. "Excuse me, but I don't think you gave me enough breakfast and I'm hungry again," he said (although it sounded more like *Yeeeeeeooowwwwwww!*)

Briony stood up and stretched. "I'm going to have a slice of toast."

"Good," Elizabeth said. "You can make the tea. I've boiled the kettle."

"Give Killer a handful of that dried cat food while you're there," I called after her, "or maybe a bowl of nails to chew on. He likes either."

"And I think you'd better ring the warehouse again," Elizabeth said to me.

221

"Don't worry. The chairs are on their way."

"I've got it!" piped up Sammi, who had gone rather quiet. "Two and two? That makes four. Fancy Briony not knowing that."

32
The Grand Opening

I could hardly sleep last night, I was so excited. The Grand Opening *and* Mum coming home. Almost too much to bear.

I was up early. Showered (yes, I know – two in one week – unheard of!) and wearing clean clothes. At least, I think they were clean. I'd lost track a bit. Anyway, they didn't smell too bad. And the bits of grit came off quite easily with a good shake.

When I walked into the PGR at eight o'clock, everyone was sitting down eating toast and munching Munchy Malcolms. There was a round of applause for my early appearance. I took a bow. You have to make the most of these moments. I say that everyone was there – everyone, of course, except for Briony. It was probably too much to expect her up this early.

Even Killer was in the kitchen, eating his breakfast of old shoes sprinkled liberally with charred biscuit.

"So," I asked, reaching for the Munchy Malcolms, "have we all enjoyed the last few weeks?"

"It wasn't quite how I imagined it would be,"

Jaz said. "I was thinking more along the lines of a party every night. Lots of dancing."

I splashed some milk on my cereal. "Lots of boys?"

Jaz poked out her tongue. "There's nothing wrong with boys. They're not all grubby and smelly like you."

I was shocked. "I'm wearing clean clothes. I've just showered!"

Everyone gasped. Jaz fell off her chair and lay on the floor groaning and waving her arms and legs in the air and yelling, "The world's gone mad! The world's gone mad!"

"A thought," Elizabeth said. "We're opening the café today. But what about tomorrow?"

"It's Sunday," Jaz said, getting up and brushing herself down. "We won't open on a Sunday, will we?"

"I think you do at the seaside," I said. "At least, you do in the summer."

"My point is this," Elizabeth went on, "What about all next week? And the week after? We go back to school then."

"Gawd," Jaz said. "Maybe I won't have to go to school. I could turn professional. Hey – there's a thought. I could be a professional chef."

"Mum'll take over," I said. "That is why we moved here isn't it? To open the café?"

"Of course it is," Elizabeth said, "It's just . . . well, she's not going to be prepared."

"We don't have to keep it open," I said. "It can be a practice run."

"Only three hours to opening time," Sammi said. "And four hours to Mum time."

"I'll drink to that." I lifted the teapot to pour a cup. "The teapot's empty!"

"You'd better put some more hot water in it, then," Jaz said.

"I'll do it." Briony appeared from the café. Briony up and dressed at ten past eight? This was indeed a special day. She had a tape measure in her hand.

"Hey, Briony," I said, "where are you going with that tape measure in your hand?"

"Well," she said, "just doing a bit of measuring. Tape measures are very useful for that kind of thing."

"But what are you measuring?"

"I'm testing out a theory," she said mysteriously. "All will be revealed."

I thought about the skeleton and the secret passage and the forgery in the art gallery and the possible murder. It wasn't only the opening of the café that

225

Mum would have to deal with. I hoped it wasn't all going to be too much of a shock for her.

"Oh, I nearly forgot," Elizabeth said. And she was grinning.

"What?"

"The chairs. They came this morning."

"Whoooooooo!" I yelled and punched the air. "What are they like?"

"I haven't looked yet," Elizabeth said. "I left the warehouse people unloading them and they offered to put them round the tables themselves."

"It's a shame we didn't have time to paint them," I said. "Never mind. Hopefully they won't look too bad. Let's go and see."

We all trooped into the café. There they were, each chair neatly stowed under a table.

"That's wonderful," I said. "They don't look too bad unpainted. You can't even see the scratches. They don't look like seconds at all – they look new."

One hour to go. Elizabeth and I had just finished hanging up a banner and balloons. The banner said *HAPPY BIRTHDAY*. Not exactly the right message, but the party shop didn't have one that said *HAPPY CAFÉ OPENING*. And so everything was ready. Everything organised. Elizabeth and I were still admiring our work when Mrs Herring arrived.

"Everyzing ready?" Mrs Herring asked, pulling out a chair to sit down.

"Yes," I said. "Everything's fine and dandy. I think everything will go very smoothly from now on."

"What's the matter?" Elizabeth asked.

Mrs Herring hadn't sat down. She was still standing and staring at her chair, looking perplexed.

"Are you OK?" I asked.

"Zis chair," Mrs Herring said. "Zere's somezing wrong viz it. Look. It doesn't have bottom."

We looked. She was right. The chair didn't have a seat. Just a wooden ring and a big hole where the bit that you sit on should be. I felt a funny feeling in my stomach.

"Oh dear," I said. "It's because the chairs are seconds. Don't worry. It's probably the only one without a bottom."

I pulled another chair out from under the table. That didn't have a bottom. Elizabeth pulled a chair out. That didn't have a seat either.

And so, with the terrible sinking feeling in my

stomach getting lower and lower and worse and worse, we looked at all the chairs in the café. Not one of them had a seat – apart from the scratched chair that the warehouse manager had shown me.

"Now what are we going to do?" I asked.

Mrs Herring shrugged. "Ask people not to sit down?"

Briony appeared, looking very excited. She was holding a photograph in her hand. "I think I've got it."

"Can you sit on it?" I asked her.

She looked confused. "Eh? What do you mean?"

"It's the chairs," I said. "They don't have bottoms."

"You're joking."

"For once," Elizabeth said, "he's not."

"What's that photograph?" I asked.

"Ah," Briony said, getting excited again, "it's the solution. The two mysteries. They're linked, and I think I've got the answer."

"What two mysteries?" Elizabeth asked.

"Yes," I said, "don't keep us in suspenders."

"OK," Briony went on, "are you ready for this?"

"Yes," I said. "Tell us."

"Look at this photo."

Briony put the picture she'd been clutching on to the table. She'd printed it out on a large sheet of paper.

It showed the wall of the café as it was after we'd cleaned up, but before we'd repainted it. In the centre was a large naked woman. I looked at it, as requested, but couldn't see anything unusual.

"Just look," Briony said. "Can't you see?"

"She looks a bit like Mrs Crabforth," I said. "Our old teacher."

Briony smiled. "The mystery of the paintings and the mystery of the ghost. I think they're related."

Elizabeth looked perplexed. "Are you saying that the ghost painted the pictures?"

"Not exactly," Briony said. "But listen. Every time we've been visited by the ghost and you've all been running around getting yourselves into tizzies. . ."

"I don't think we have been getting into tizzies," I said. "I would never get into a tizzy."

"Shush," Elizabeth said.

"Tizzies don't suit me."

"Do you want to hear this, or don't you?" Briony said.

"Sorry," I said.

"Right. . . so. . . All along I've said there's no such thing as ghosts. But the sound we heard was real. So, I asked myself – what was it? And where was it actually coming from? Then it came to me. It's a sound

229

we hear all the time. I was amazed I hadn't thought of it before. I'm amazed that none of you knew what it was either."

"Go on," I urged.

"Seagulls," Briony said.

"That's it?" I said. "Seagulls?"

Briony nodded.

"There aren't any seagulls in the house. I'm sure we would have noticed a seagull sitting down to breakfast."

Briony sighed. "Come on. Don't be thick. Seagulls nest in chimneys. We had a seagull nesting in the chimney. The sound carries down the flue. At night it sounds like a ghost. Simple."

"Well, that does make sense," I had to agree. "Well, whaddya know. A seagull, eh?"

"So you're saying that the ghostly seagull *stole* the paintings," Elizabeth said.

"Well, assuming it is John Montague's body – and assuming he did forge those paintings and they are still hidden in the house. . ."

"I still think it's unlikely," I said.

"Vat do you mean?" Mrs Herring asked sharply. "Body? Vot is it about body?"

Oh dear. I'd forgotten Mrs Herring was there. And

we hadn't told her about the skeleton, let alone that we thought it might be John Montague.

Briony hesitated. "Oh . . . er . . . nothing. Anyway, the important thing is – if the paintings are here – I think I know where they might be."

We stared at her. Well, I know Briony is bright. But this seemed to be beyond brightness. If she knew where the paintings were, it would be a stroke of genius.

"Paintings? Body? Vot is going on?" Mrs Herring asked.

"Um. . . We'll explain in a minute," I said, "it's a bit complicated."

"Now, where was I?" Briony said. "Oh yes. Once I'd figured out what the ghost was – the noise of a baby seagull crying and the squawk of its mother echoing down the chimney – I began to wonder where the chimney was."

"What do you mean?" Elizabeth asked. "There are lots of chimneys. There are fireplaces all over the house."

"But none in this room," Briony said. "None in the café. Surely an old building like this – an inn – would have had a fireplace in its biggest room? You know, with big logs on. And a spit for roasting meat, perhaps. So, where is it?"

"I've got it!" I said. "The fireplace in here has been boarded over. Why? Because that's where John Montague hid the paintings."

"Correct." Briony said.

"Just because the fireplace has been boarded over," Elizabeth said, "doesn't mean the paintings are there. Lots of people block up fireplaces. And even if he did hide them, they could be anywhere in the house."

"Not really," Briony said. "If the killer knew that the paintings were there, he'd have searched the house pretty thoroughly. It would have to be a very good hiding place."

"Maybe," Elizabeth said, "but it's all guesswork. First of all we find a skeleton. . ."

"Now you have skeleton also?" Mrs Herring interrupted.

"We found a secret passage in the cellar," I told her. "And it led to a room with a skeleton in it. We know that John Montague disappeared so we wondered if the skeleton was him."

"But we don't know it's him," Elizabeth said. "It could be anyone. It could have been there for hundreds of years. And the pictures – we don't know for sure they were stolen. And even if they were, it's unlikely they'd still be in this house."

"But look at the photo again," Briony urged.

We looked.

"You must see it now," she said.

"I do!" Elizabeth yelled.

"Well, I don't," I said.

"Look! It's there. Look!" Elizabeth was jumping up and down.

"Where? Where?" I was getting cross. But then I saw it too. The fat lady who looked like Mrs Crabforth was pointing. She was definitely pointing. And when you followed the line of her finger, there was nothing there. Not on the wall, anyway.

"She's pointing," I said.

"That's right. At the hidden fireplace."

"But why would John Montague hide the paintings in the fireplace, board it over and then paint a picture of someone pointing at the hiding place?"

Briony shrugged. "I don't know."

"In case something happened to him?" Elizabeth asked.

"But *is* she pointing at the chimney?" I asked.

"Let's go and see," Briony said. "If there's no fireplace there, then I'll agree with Elizabeth. It's all guesswork and we're wasting our time."

"But if there is. . ." I said.

We followed her across to the wall and Briony began tapping. Sure enough, right where the fat lady's finger had been pointing, there was a hollow sound.

We all stood and stared. On the other side of that wall there could be paintings worth thousands of pounds. And, I suddenly realised, there was bound to be a huge reward for them.

"What's going on?" It was Jaz, with Sammi in tow. "Why are you all standing there staring at the wall?

"Because," I said, "thanks to Briony's amazing detective work, we think there are paintings on the other side of that wall that are worth a fortune."

"You're joking," Jaz said.

"No, really," I said.

"You *are* joking, aren't you?"

"No, he's not," Elizabeth said.

"Well, let's find out if there's anything there," Jaz said.

"We can't," I said. "Everyone will be arriving soon. We open in. . ." I glanced at the clock, "exactly fifty minutes. It will have to wait."

"How can it wait?" Elizabeth said. "We can't go through the café opening, serving customers and saying hello to Mum, if all the time we know there might be all that money on the other side of the wall."

"Paintings," I said. "Not money. There is a difference."

"Ve do have time," Mrs Herring said. "Ve could cut hole in vall and take look before anyone arrives."

"But we can't cut a hole in the middle of my genius artwork," I protested.

"Of course we can," Elizabeth said.

"I'll go and get a hammer and some tools," Jaz yelled, and ran off.

"Well, I'm not sure," I said.

"We can put something up against it to hide the hole," Elizabeth said.

"Yes," Briony said. "I've just the thing." And she disappeared too.

"Zis is so exciting, isn't it?" Mrs Herring said. "I zink I'll have to pop to loo."

Briony reappeared first. She was holding the giant frame of collaged photos that she'd made.

"We'll just make sure the hole is smaller than the frame," she said, "then we can lean the frame against it to hide the hole."

"Where's Jaz?" It was Sandy. She was wearing a red and pink apron with SLAVE written on it and holding a large lettuce. "We need her in the kitchen."

"She'll be back in a second," Elizabeth said.

"What's going on?" Sandy asked. "And why don't the chairs have bottoms?"

Sammi started giggling.

"It's not funny," I said.

Jaz returned lugging Dad's bag of tools. I hunted around and found a big hammer, a bit rusty, and a large, flat chisel. Then I set to work as carefully as I could.

"Hurry up," Jaz said.

Mrs Herring returned. "Vait for me!"

"What *is* going on?" Sandy asked again.

"It's a kind of treasure hunt," Briony said.

"If Montague *did* board up the fireplace to make a hiding place for stolen paintings," I said, "wouldn't he have made a secret door of some kind, to get them in or out?"

"I thought of that," Briony agreed. "I think there *is* a way in – but I can't find it."

I carefully dug out a large section of the plasterboard. There was, indeed, a fireplace behind it. I reached in and felt around in the darkness.

Amazingly, I could feel something. A package of some kind. I carefully pulled it out and laid it on the floor. It was rolled up, about half a metre long, clad in some kind of rubbery material. I undid the cords and carefully unwrapped it. I was holding my breath. And there it was: *Red Square* by Kazimir Malevich.

"Wow!" Sammi said.

We all stared.

I felt around some more, and pulled out three more packages, all wrapped in the same way. But before I could open them, someone spoke from behind us.

"Clever children. Now, hand those paintings over to us."

We spun round. Two men stood behind us. They looked dark and sinister framed against the bright light of the café windows. The man who had spoken was holding a gun. He was pointing it straight at me.

33
Hostage Situation

Frank Meek, gun in hand, was smiling at us. Not in a pleasant way. And beside him was Ironhead. But I couldn't believe that Ironhead would do us any harm. He was a friend. He'd even given me a CD of his band. Then I remembered that he'd once dropped a heavy speaker cabinet on someone's head.

My mouth was dry and I could feel my heart thudding. You read about guns and robberies and violence and it sounds exciting. But having a gun pointed at you . . . it was very, very scary.

"You heard me," Frank said. "Hand over the loot."

Hand over the loot? It was like something out of a bad detective movie. I stood frozen to the spot, like one of those street entertainers that look like statues until you put money in their hat.

"Go on, then," Elizabeth told me.

I took a deep breath. Then I nodded, and gingerly wrapped the *Red Square* up again. I was thinking. Finding the paintings meant that the skeleton really was John Montague, after all. And it looked as if he'd been murdered by the man who was now pointing a gun at me.

"Hurry up!"

"How did you know we'd found the pictures?" Briony asked him.

Frank grinned. "That'd be telling, wouldn't it."

But how could the men have known? We'd only just found the paintings. Those two must have been on their way here while I was knocking a hole in the wall. It was weird. Maybe they'd planted some sort of listening device. Yes, that would make sense. And if they knew we'd found the paintings, then they'd probably know that we'd unearthed the skeleton, too. Would they kill us just to keep us quiet?

I handed over the paintings.

"Now, this is what you are going to do," Frank said. "You are going to sit down and put your hands on your heads. . ."

"We can't," Elizabeth said.

"What?" Frank pointed his gun at Elizabeth.

"The chairs don't work," Elizabeth said.

"Eh?"

"The chairs. They haven't got bottoms."

There was a few seconds' silence while Frank inspected the chairs.

"OK, then," he said. "In that case, turn round and face the wall. Start counting. When you reach one hundred, we'll be gone."

This was nonsense. As soon as they left the café, we'd be on the phone. And the police would soon catch them. A busy bank holiday weekend at a seaside resort? They wouldn't get very far. They'd be stuck in traffic before they even reached the ring road.

We turned around to face the wall as instructed.

"One more thing," said Frank. "While you are counting, I want you to sing a song."

Sing a song? What was he on about now?

"What song?" Sammi asked.

"You choose," Frank said.

"How about 'The Meteorite That Obliterated The Planet Earth'?" I suggested.

"Don't be funny," Frank said.

"That's not a funny song," Ironhead said, "it's dead serious. It was our closing number. . ."

"Shut up," Frank said.

"What happened to the chairs, then?" Ironhead asked.

"Shut it!" Frank shouted.

"How about 'The Wheels on the Bus'?" Sammi suggested.

"I think we should sing an Amber Lite song," Jaz said.

"I don't know the words to any Amber Lite songs," Elizabeth said.

"You must know 'My Boyfriend's Better Than Your Boyfriend'," Jaz said. "It was number one for. . ."

"Shut up!" Frank yelled.

I tried to think of a song we all knew. I looked up and noticed the banner strung across the ceiling. "How about 'Happy Birthday'? We all know the words to that."

"Sing 'Happy Birthday', then," Frank said. "Now!"

"But whose birthday is it?" Sammi asked.

"Mine!" Frank said. "And thanks for the present. Now sing – or someone gets shot."

We started singing "Happy birthday to you".

"Louder," Frank said.

We sang louder.

After the last "happy birthday to you", I wondered if they'd gone yet. It was difficult to count and sing at the same time.

"Who is Frank, I wonder?"

We stopped singing and turned round. There stood Inspector Carpet.

"Thank God," said Elizabeth. "Did you get them?"

The inspector looked blank. "Did I get who, young lady?"

"Frank and Ironhead!" Elizabeth cried. "You must have seen them. You must have passed them coming in. They've only just gone."

"What on earth are you talking about? And why were you all standing facing the wall and singing 'Happy Birthday'?" the inspector asked.

"Listen carefully," Briony said, trying to speak slowly and evenly, although her voice was trembling. "We have just found, hidden behind this wall, several stolen paintings. Paintings stolen from the art gallery."

"What stolen paintings? There haven't been any more robberies. I'd have heard about it."

"Remember the Russian icons that were stolen and then recovered?" Briony said, "Well, you didn't get everyone, did you? Only the actual thief."

"There was some talk about. . ." the inspector began.

"Listen. I think the same gang have been substituting forgeries for paintings in the gallery. The paintings were hidden here. But the gang members have taken them. . . They held us up at gunpoint. We haven't got time to explain everything. They are getting away. Do something, please. . ." Briony sounded exasperated.

I couldn't believe that Frank and Ironhead had got past Inspector Carpet without being noticed. Then I realised why.

"The cellar!" I cried. "The secret passage! That's why we had to make all that noise. So we didn't hear which way they went. They took the secret passage."

The inspector looked at me blankly. "Now you really are talking in riddles."

Elizabeth gave a little scream.

"What's up?" I asked.

"Sammi," she said. "Where's Sammi? Oh, no. . ."

"They've got Sammi," Jaz wailed.

"They've got Sammi?" the inspector repeated.

"Please listen," I said. "A gang has stolen some valuable paintings. They have kidnapped our little sister, Sammi. There's a secret passage under this house. It must lead somewhere. Maybe to the beach, if it was used for smuggling. They're getting away. You are a police officer. . ."

The inspector straightened up. "I certainly am," he said. He looked suddenly more alert. At last he seemed to have grasped what was going on. "Right, how many are there in the gang?"

"Two. Frank Meek and Ironhead."

"Only two?" The inspector looked a little disappointed.

"They've got a gun," I added.

"A gun? A gun, eh? Oh, well, that's different. That's good!"

"Hurry! For God's sake!" Jaz shouted.

We rushed down to the cellar. Unlike the inspector, I thought the fact that they had a gun was a bad thing. A very bad thing.

The inspector spoke on his mobile as we stood in the darkness staring at the doorway to the secret passage. The big old press was lying tipped on its side. Briony appeared with the torch.

"Yes," the inspector was saying. "I most certainly will. I certainly won't. OK . . . I certainly will. No . . . I most certainly won't. Don't worry. Yes, I certainly will." He put the phone back in his pocket. "They're sending every available officer. And a helicopter. And the coastguard has been alerted."

"Come on," Jaz shouted. "Let's follow them."

"Wait," I said. "People are going to be arriving upstairs soon. Our guests. No one will be there to welcome them."

"Kavita is there," Jaz said.

I groaned. "You can't leave Kavita on her own. She'll

244

wonder what's happened. She'll think we've all been abducted by aliens or something."

"Come on," Jaz said, and started climbing through the small doorway.

"Wait," Elizabeth said, "Wilf's right. Someone will have to look after the café. And be there when the police arrive. You stay here, Sandy. . ."

"And I vill, too," Mrs Herring said. "Don't vorry. I vill look after café."

"Let's go, then," Jaz yelled.

"I'm afraid you can't," the inspector said. "They've got a gun. You will *all* have to wait here. I'll go."

But it was too late, Jaz had already disappeared into the darkness and Briony was close behind her with the torch.

"Come back," the inspector shouted. "I forbid you to go."

"Sammi's our sister," Elizabeth said, close on Briony's heels. "We've got to get her back."

"I'll have to arrest you. . ."

"Very funny," I said, following Elizabeth through the doorway.

"It's not funny," I heard him say, as he squeezed his huge frame through the small opening behind me.

There was a scream. It was Jaz. I'd forgotten that we hadn't told her about the skeleton. And there it was – still slouched against the wall of the small storeroom.

We calmed her down as best we could and quickly explained to her and the inspector how we had found it. The other door to the storeroom was now open, the bolts drawn back.

As everyone climbed through the door and into the darkness of the passage beyond, I paused for a moment, glanced back at the skeleton and glimpsed something on the floor, just under the skeleton's ribcage. I reached forward and picked it up. A bullet.

I put the bullet in my pocket, clambered through the doorway and followed the flickering torchlight into the tunnel.

As we hurried along the passageway, the torch cast pools of brightness and black shadows across the brick roof and the rough stone floor. Our feet splashed though puddles and crunched over shells and pebbles.

"What's that?" the inspector cried.

Now the tunnel narrowed and began twisting this way and that. It was much harder to keep together and the floor had become rocky and uneven. Two points of light, the eyes of some ferocious sea-monster, perhaps, glowed from a dark recess. A malevolent creature materialised before us.

"Careful," the inspector said. "It's some kind of wild animal."

"You're right," Elizabeth said. "It's Killer."

"Killer? There's a killer blocking our path?"

"It's our cat."

"Cat? It looks more like a lion."

More like a tiger, I thought. One of those big white Siberian tigers.

"Get a move on," Jaz cried.

We followed the inspector, with Killer padding along behind us.

"Listen," Briony said. We listened. "You can hear the sea quite clearly. And smell the salty air. We must be getting close."

We were moving more slowly now, negotiating the twisting tunnel. This was some kind of natural rock formation. To think that smugglers brought their contraband through here hundreds of years ago! No sign of any abandoned bottles of rum, though.

"Look," Briony said. "Light."

She turned the torch off. Sure enough, we were no

longer in pitch darkness. There was a faint glow ahead of us.

We followed the inspector round a last bend and we could see the light source at floor level. We squeezed through a gap beneath a rocky overhang and into a small cave. The floor was covered in seaweed. It felt like walking on a squashy mattress. Thousands of tiny, disturbed flies began buzzing around our legs. And in front of us there was a vertical strip of blinding light just wide enough to squeeze through.

"Looks like they moved that boulder out of the way," Briony said.

With some difficulty, the inspector squeezed through and we followed. Daylight! It was good to be in the open air again.

The tunnel, as I'd expected, came out at the cliffs. We looked around. You could hear shouts and the chatter of holidaymakers making the most of the unusual morning sunshine. A few families were fishing in rock pools for crabs.

I could hear a helicopter. Hopefully, that was the police.

"There they are!" yelled Elizabeth.

We rushed down to the water's edge, slipping and

sliding over the weed-covered rocks, negotiating pools of water.

We stopped. The two men had a boat but were obviously having trouble with it. Just as well, or they'd be gone by now. Ironhead was fiddling with the engine and swearing. Frank was holding Sammi, his arm locked around her.

"Don't come any closer," Frank yelled, "or I'll shoot the girl."

We stopped at the edge of the small sandy strip of beach. We were about ten metres from the boat.

"You wouldn't shoot a little girl," the inspector shouted. "Now, stop being silly. Let her go."

"Back off," Frank said.

"There's a difference between murder and robbery," the inspector said. "Let her go. You can't escape. You must see that."

"This is your last chance," Frank said, and he waved the gun towards us. "Now, back off."

I wondered what we could do. Maybe I could dive for the gun and grab it before Frank fired. No, that would be stupid. Somebody would get hurt. Above our heads a seagull swooped and let out a loud, piercing cry of alarm.

With a splutter and a roar, the little motor on the boat came to life.

"Let's go!" Ironhead yelled.

As Frank turned, Sammi let out a piercing scream and started kicking him.

There was a sudden hissing, snarling noise and a streak of white hurtled through the air. Killer leapt, landing on Frank's face and propelling him backwards into the sea. Sammi fell sideways into the boat, Frank hit the water with a huge splash and the gun went flying into the air.

The rest was easy.

34
The Other Grand Opening

The opening was a huge success. Mrs Ems took our photos, and a picture of the hole where the painting had been found, and interviewed us. Then she tucked into a huge pile of bat-cakes. These were little chocolate sponges with two flat slivers of chocolate stuck in the top like a bat's wings and a blob of cream on top. We were going to get a very good write-up in the *Town Crier*, I reckoned.

A doctor came to look at Sammi, but she seemed fine, despite having been captured at gunpoint. While we'd been chasing the villains through the tunnel and saving Sammi and the paintings on the beach, Mrs Herring and Jaz's mates had been busy rearranging the furniture. They'd taken the useless chairs out, stacked them in the yard and put the tables around the edge of the café. Then they'd put all the food out on the tables to make a buffet. It looked really professional. There were Spiderman dips and a new batch of Kryptonite Krackers, as well as Cat Woman Crisps and The Riddler sausage rolls, with little riddles stuck in them like fortune cookies. And desserts – Silver Surfer Strawberry Fool and Peach and Chocolate Bat Cave Surprise. Jaz and her friends had produced quite a spread.

A lot of people had turned up – mainly holidaymakers, but some locals, too – and there was a warm and excited buzz about the place. But all the time we were watching the clock and the door for Mum.

"Well done," Inspector Carpet said. "So, all those paintings hanging in the gallery are forgeries? Who'd have thought it? And now we've caught the gang – well, two of them, anyway – with the stolen paintings. Not to mention a charge of kidnapping and murder."

"That *is* John Montague's skeleton, then?" I asked.

"It's been taken to the lab," the inspector said. "But I think I can safely say, without too much fear of contradiction and without too much of a risk of getting egg on my face or . . . um . . . trifle on my shoes that – yes, I'm pretty much convinced, maybe as much as seventy-three per cent, that it is him."

"But I don't think those men murdered anyone," Sammi said.

The inspector smiled. "Now don't you worry about

that, young missy, you've had a bit of a shock, what with being kidnapped and, you know . . . seeing the skeleton."

"The skeleton was a bit scary," Sammi said. "But those two men didn't do it."

"I think we'll find they did," the inspector said.

"No, they didn't. They were talking about it. Arguing about it." Sammi was insistent.

"Arguing?" the inspector said.

"Yes. Frank was saying that John deserved it and Ironhead was saying that nobody deserved that. Then Frank said that he didn't kill him, anyway. It was the boss."

"The boss?" the inspector said. "Well . . . when the Russian icons were stolen we figured there was a driver . . . that would be the Meek character . . . and someone working on the inside. . ."

"John Montague," I said.

"But there were others involved," Briony said. "Ironhead, for a start. But I'm sure he's not the boss."

"I've got it!" I said. "When we were making a hole in the wall to get the painting out, the gang appeared. How did they know? They must have planted a listening device. So, who do we know who's good at doing that sort of thing?"

"Oh no – Thumbs, when he did the wiring," Elizabeth said. "And do you remember his real name?"

We looked at her blankly.

"His real name is Ivan! It's a Russian name."

"And they were all Russian paintings!" I said.

"Hello, you lot."

We all jumped.

"It seems to be going well. Lots of people." Thumbs was holding a cup of tea.

"Talk of the Devil," I said.

"What? What's that?" Thumbs said.

"Here's the other gang member," I told the inspector. "Ivan! Alias Thumbs! He's the boss!"

"What? I'm the . . . oops!" As Thumbs turned, his cup slid off the saucer and crashed to the floor. Hot tea splashed everywhere.

"Sorry," Thumbs said. "You made me jump."

Elizabeth picked up the broken pieces. "I'll get a mop."

"It's not Thumbs," Briony said. "There's no listening device."

"I didn't think it was," Thumbs said, sounding relieved. "I think I'd have known, if I was the boss."

"Do you deny being Russian?" the inspector demanded.

"Yeah. I come from Stepney."

"Oh," said the inspector.

"What happened to the chairs?" Thumbs asked.

"Hello," Mrs Herring said. She was wearing an apron over her smart suit, with a big smiley face. "All going vell, da?"

"It certainly is," Elizabeth said.

"Ven's your mum turning up, zen?"

"Any time now," Elizabeth said.

"How exciting. Ve meet your mum at last. Now, can I get you anyzing? Anozer drink? Tea?"

"What I'd like," Thumbs said, "is a coffee. Nice and strong. I've had a nasty shock. I was nearly a criminal. I was nearly the boss."

"Anyone else vant tea or coffee?" Mrs Herring asked.

"We're OK, thanks," Elizabeth said.

Mrs Herring disappeared with the order.

"But Briony knows who the boss is," I said. "Don't you, Briony?"

Briony smiled. "Of course I do. It's obvious. The clues have been there all along."

"It's all right for you lot." Jaz looked hot and

bothered. "Standing around enjoying yourself. It's hard work in the kitchen. Isn't it about time someone else took a turn?"

"You're doing a great job," I said.

"Briony was about to tell us. . ." Elizabeth began. But at that moment Sammi let out a loud shriek.

"Look, look. It's Mum!"

All heads turned her way. Then everyone jumped up and ran to the door. I'd imagined that we'd all be sitting having a drink and a batburger when Mum appeared, and we'd act all nonchalant and say, "What? The café? Oh yes . . . we thought we'd open it. It's doing very well. . ." You know, be cool.

Mum had two big suitcases and a stuffed Spanish donkey under her arm. "*Hola, mi bambinos,*" she cried, her arms flung open wide. And everyone rushed to be first to reach her. There was lots of hugging and kissing. I made my way over and gave her a hug. It was a wonderful feeling, having her back. Everyone was crying. I don't know what the customers thought.

Mum looked a bit shell-shocked. She kept looking round and saying, "Goodness gracious!" and "Blooming heck!" These are her two favourite expressions. It was good to hear them again.

"The café," she said. "I don't believe it. What. . ."

"Have *we* got things to tell you," I said.

"And not just about the café," Elizabeth said.

"What do you mean? Wow! Look at the walls. Did you do that, Wilf?"

"I did," I said.

"It's great . . . fantastic! Where's Dad?"

"There's someone you must meet," I said. We led Mum to the back of the café and introduced her to Inspector Carpet and Thumbs.

"You have a bunch of very clever children," the inspector said.

"I know," Mum replied.

"How's the abseiling going?"

Mum gave him a blank look.

"I'd like to climb Everest some time," the Inspector said.

"That's nice," she said, bewildered.

"Don't worry, Mum," I said. And we started to tell her about the café and Dad going away and the hidden paintings and that there would probably be a reward. And she looked even more shell-shocked. And she said "Goodness gracious!" a few more times and "Blooming heck!" again.

"What you need," Thumbs said, "is a nice cuppa."

"I'll go," Jaz said. "I'd better check that everything's

OK in the kitchen and that Kavita and Sandy aren't being overwhelmed. Cup of tea, Mum?"

"Yes, please. A cup of tea. A real English one. They're not very good at tea in Spain."

"And you could find out where my coffee's got to," Thumbs said.

Mum sighed. "And I could do with a sit-down."

"We had a bit of a problem with the chairs," Elizabeth said.

"I'll fetch a chair from the PGR," I said.

Jaz reappeared with a cup of tea for Mum and Thumbs' coffee. "I had to make it," Jaz said. "Mrs Herring's disappeared."

"What?" Briony cried. "Oh, no!"

"She's probably in the loo."

"We mustn't let her get away," Briony cried. "Come on, Inspector."

"What?" The inspector looked perplexed – yet again.

"After her," Briony said again. "You mustn't let Mrs Herring get away."

"Mrs Herring?" I said. "Are you saying that Mrs Herring is involved? You think she's a member of the gang?"

"Of course she's involved. John Montague was

the forger, and the man on the inside. No doubt he masterminded the theft of the Russian icons, but it all went wrong. One man was caught and he's still in prison. Frank Meek was the driver. Ironhead was . . . well, the muscle. That's four. And the fifth? Mrs Herring, of course. She isn't just a gang member. She's the boss."

"Who's Mrs Herring?" Mum asked.

"She's a killer," Briony said. "That's who. You all stay with Mum. Inspector – come with me. Did anyone notice if she went out of the café? No, I didn't think so."

Elizabeth and I rushed after the inspector and Briony as they ran through the PGR. Briony grabbed the torch and started to sprint down the steps to the cellar. Suddenly she stopped. We all slid to a halt on the steps behind her and peered downwards.

Mrs Herring hadn't got far. There she was, standing in the corner of the cellar. And in front of her, hissing and spitting, stood Killer.

"Get zat cat away from me!"

"That's twice Killer's saved the day," I said. "That cat should get a medal. But I can't believe Mrs Herring's the boss of the gang."

"I can," Elizabeth said.

"Gang boss? Zat's rubbish," Mrs Herring said. "I don't know vat you're talking about."

"I think you do," Briony said. "Why did you come to see us in the first place? You said you were a neighbour, but you're not."

"Of course I am."

"You're not. You don't even live in this town. At least, there's no Mrs Herring on the electoral roll. That's a record of everybody in the town over the age of eighteen who's allowed to vote. I checked with the council. And I don't believe you're a cleaner, either."

"I just didn't register zis year, zat's all. And I am cleaner. I told you. I have to earn money somehow."

"Rubbish," Briony cried. "You came to us because you suspected the paintings were still here, didn't you? You hoped they were, anyway, and it was worth a try. You wanted to be our cleaner so that you could snoop around without anyone being suspicious." Briony took a breath. "And you knew about the skeleton – because you killed John Montague, didn't you? All that rubbish about a murder hundreds of years ago, that was just a ploy to stop us exploring the cellar. You didn't want us discovering the secret passage. So you encouraged us to think that the cellar was haunted.

"And your plan worked. You did scare us off – you

and the seagulls with their screeching in the night. But there never was any murder hundreds of years ago, was there? There was just the one you committed five years ago. And in the end, we *did* find the secret passageway. And we *did* find the skeleton. And we *did* find the paintings."

"Zat's all rubbish." Mrs Herring was shaking her head and looking outraged.

Briony took a deep breath. "Also, you said that you didn't know John Montague very well. But then you let slip that he had a great sense of humour."

"That doesn't prove anyzing."

"That's right," the inspector said, "that doesn't mean she's a murderer."

"No, it doesn't," Briony went on, "but it got me thinking. And then I happened upon something very interesting."

"What?"

"Something in your handbag."

"Vat?" Mrs Herring screeched. "You've been looking in my handbag? How dare you?"

"Not on purpose," Briony said. "But Killer stole it and . . . well, it was sort of open and there was your purse and I couldn't help glancing at your credit cards and, well, you seem to have quite a few in the name of Valentina Petrova. So, I went back through all the newspaper reports that I'd been researching for the Comic Café website and your name came up several times. You *did* know John Montague. You worked with him when he was buying works of art for the gallery. You were advising the gallery on the purchase of a set of six Russian icons."

"Vat if I vas? Zat still doesn't prove anyzing," Mrs Herring said.

"Valentina Petrova?" The inspector scratched his head. "That name rings a bell. I remember reading the name when I was tying up the loose ends after the burglary. It will all be in the records."

"You are ridiculous. Now remove zat vicious brute," Mrs Herring said, "and let me go." Killer was still crouching in front of her, glaring at her with mean eyes. "It's all lies. My name iz Herring. I've never heard of Valentina Petrova."

Briony moved down the steps to stand in front of Mrs Herring in the cellar. We all followed. "Then show us your credit cards," Briony said, "and prove it. Valentina Petrova is a Russian name."

"So it's not me. I have told you. I am Polish."

Briony shook her head. "You say 'da', which is Russian for yes. 'Yes' in Polish is 'tak'!"

"I'm confused," Elizabeth said.

"OK," Briony said patiently. "This is what I think. Petrova, alias Mrs Herring, art criminal, acts as adviser to John Montague when he shows an interest in buying a set of six Russian icons for the gallery. Then she persuades Montague to get a gang together to steal the icons. She knows she can sell them for a huge amount of money back in Russia. The robbery goes wrong, the thief gets caught, but the rest of them get away and the icons go back to the gallery."

"Go on," I said.

"Well, Petrova and Montague don't want to give up now. So they hatch another plan. Petrova advises the gallery to acquire more Russian works. Montague, a pretty good artist, will forge copies, which he'll substitute for the originals in the gallery. He has access at all times. He's a trustee, remember.

"And this plan works. Over time, Montague buys several 20th-century Russian paintings for the gallery. He makes professional-looking copies and swaps them for the real paintings. Nobody notices the forgeries – after all, Montague and Petrova are the gallery's art experts.

"Our suspicions were raised when you spotted his

tiny mistake, Wilf – he copied one painting, *Red Square*, back to front."

"Thank you." I gave a little bow.

"Petrova arrives to pick up the latest batch of original paintings – and something happens. Maybe there's an argument. Maybe Montague wants more money." She turned to Mrs Herring, who was staring hard at the ground. "Whatever it was, Montague doesn't hand over the paintings. He's hidden them in the fireplace by plastering it over.

"And Petrova kills him. Perhaps on purpose, perhaps by mistake." Briony paused. Mrs Herring remained silent. She wasn't giving anything away, so Briony went on: "She hides the body in the secret tunnel. But – she can't find the paintings!

"Then we come along. Petrova, calling herself Mrs Herring, wants to keep an eye on us. She is nervous. We might find the body. So she warns us away from the cellar, making up a story about a ghost and a murder that never happened. And she's never given up hope of one day finding the paintings. And guess what?"

"We find them for her," I said.

"But how come Meek and Ironhead turned up right on time to take them from us?" I asked.

"Maybe they were involved in the forgeries scam,"

Briony said. "Or maybe Mrs Herring thought they'd be useful to have around."

"I saw them together in a café," I said. "Mrs Herring and Frank Meek! I was on my way to the gallery."

"So, while Jaz is fetching the tools and I am fetching the collage to hide the hole that we are about to make in the wall, Mrs Herring says she's going to the loo – but really she phones her heavies, who come straight round. The call will be logged on her mobile," Briony said, turning to the inspector.

"We'll soon see." The inspector reached for Mrs Herring's handbag.

"And take a look at her credit cards while you're about it," Briony said.

"Come on, then, show me," the inspector said.

Mrs Herring hugged the bag to her body. "You need varrant."

"No, I don't." He grabbed the bag and pulled. But she wouldn't let go. The inspector tugged. The bag fell open and the contents scattered all over the floor. There was a clunk. And there, lying on the cellar floor, was a gun.

We all stared at it.

"And how do you explain that?" the inspector asked.

Then I remembered. I felt in my pocket. "Would this be important?" I asked. "It was on the floor by the skeleton." And I held up the bullet I'd found.

"Hmm," the inspector said, looking from the bullet to the gun, "I wonder if they match?"

35
The Second Best Ending

Then Dad came home. We threw a big party. Mum and Dad made up. And suddenly we were rich because of the reward money and we didn't have to go to school again. Instead we had private tuition, mainly on the beach. And as a special dispensation, I didn't have to learn maths. Especially long division. The weather improved, too. The following few weeks were hot and sunny.

Perhaps that's stretching the truth – the bit about the hot weather. Things didn't exactly end like that. Actually, there wasn't any reward. We had to start at our new schools. And I still had to battle with maths.

The most amazing thing of all was the discovery that *all* the Russian 20th-century paintings in the gallery were forgeries, including *Red Square* and the Kandinsky. Experts checked every painting and it took some time. It turned out that in the three years between the robbery that went wrong and John Montague going missing, fourteen pictures had been stolen and replaced by forgeries. Good ones, too. In the end, we found another painting in the fireplace, making five in all. The others had probably gone back to Russia, sold by Mrs Herring – or rather, Ms Petrova – on the black market.

I did feel pleased with myself, I confess. It was a fluke that I'd noticed the mistake in the *Red Square* painting. And that Mrs Herring, when she destroyed Montague's studio where he made the forgeries (as she must surely have done) neglected to check that there wasn't still a slide in the slide projector.

We made the news big time. This funny old seaside town, where nothing happens, was suddenly in all the national papers and on the telly. In fact, we were international news. The publicity certainly helped the café and we were full all the following week.

We were able to stay open because Mum knew a cook who was looking for work, and a couple of people turned up on the Monday and asked if they could be waitresses. And we bought a new set of chairs. Mum was really pleased with what we'd done and couldn't believe how we'd got it together. She said she was very proud of us. It had all been down to me, she said, and I got a huge hug. Well, it was my idea, but everyone had helped. She did mention that I should, perhaps, have phoned Granny, but she didn't go on about it.

Sammi got the Spanish donkey, although she didn't have it for long. She made the mistake of taking Pedro, as she named him, to bed with her. In the morning he'd gone. He must have walked off in the night. Or been captured by the ghost. Or possibly – and this was Briony's theory – been taken away by a jealous cat. "Kevin would never do that," Sammi had said. "Of course not," we'd all agreed, and we never told her about the shredded raffia we found in the yard.

Mrs Herring was arrested for the murder of John Montague. She was, of course, Valentina Petrova. The bullet I'd found by the skeleton matched the gun in her handbag. She went on protesting her innocence, so we never discovered why she did it. She was also charged with stealing the paintings. There was no evidence to link Frank Meek and Ironhead with the original robbery or the forgeries, although everyone was sure they were involved, but they were charged with kidnapping Sammi and having a gun without a licence.

And Dad? Well, he came home the following

week. He was riding a motorbike. A Harley Davidson Sportster. Bright yellow. He wasn't wearing a Hell's Angel's get-up, though, which was one good thing. He was amazed by our efforts.

The café was full and everyone was busy. We were sitting in the PGR, drinking tea. Dad was hunting around for a spoon. Something caught his eye. "What's that? On the mantelpiece?"

It was the brown envelope he'd given me all that time ago. It was still there. He took it down and put it in his jacket pocket. "That'll come in handy," he said.

"What?" I asked.

"Oh, the cash I left for Mum. Not much. About thirty quid. It'll go towards my ferry ticket. It was all I had on me when I wrote the note giving her the address of my friend in France."

"So, if we'd opened it, we would have been able to get in touch with you right from the start?"

"Yes, of course."

I suddenly realised what he'd said.

"Dad, are you going back to France?"

"Yes," he said. "Just for a while. Some unfinished business."

"You are coming back, aren't you?" I asked.

"Of course I am," he said. "Look . . . don't worry. I shall only be there for a while. And you can come out and see me."

So Dad's going away again. We're all a bit sad, but Mum says he'll be back, and Sammi is getting really excited about the prospect of a French holiday. When Dad told her, she said, "That's good. I'll be able to spend my Euros. I tried to give them to Wilf to pay for the chairs and things, but he didn't want them." We all laughed, thinking, "Silly Sammi and her handful of Euros."

"How many Euros have you got, then," I asked her.

"Two hundred and eighty-eight."

If only we'd asked before!

Thud. Thud. Thud. What was that? I opened my eyes. Someone . . . or something was knocking on the door. I got up and pulled on my dressing-gown. "Who is it?" I asked. Silence. I crept over to the door and opened it. The landing was deserted. I walked out and looked around. The house

was quiet. Then I glimpsed something over my shoulder. I spun round. A wave of fear enveloped me. There it stood, its teeth set in a yellow grin, its eyes red and staring, its black claw reaching towards me. I had the key in my hand, but I was loath to hand it over.

I tried to escape down the stairs. But there, climbing the stairs as I knew it would be, was the Gargoyle. It began to laugh. Vampyre joined in, the two monsters laughing louder and louder.

Vampyre took Gargoyle's hand. "It's only us," it said. And it pulled the mask from its head to reveal – Dad. And when the Gorgoyle pulled its mask off – there was Mum.

And when I woke, I didn't feel scared any more.

Roger Stevens has written several novels
for young people and more than 20 books of poems.
He lives in England and in France. When he's in Brighton
he can often be found on the beach writing stories.
When he's in France he sits by a fig tree and dreams up
ideas. The rest of the time he visits schools, libraries,
festivals and museums performing and talking about his
work. Roger plays in the band *Damn Right I Got the Blues*
with the actress and author Floella Benjamin and the
writer Ken Follett, and performed the music for
Floella Benjamin's *Hey Diddle Diddle* on BBC Radio 7.
His award-winning website, *The Poetry Zone*
(www.poetryzone.co.uk) publishes poems by children
from all over the world. He performed his verse novel for
teenagers, *The Diary of Danny Chaucer* (Orion) as a play on
BBC Radio Four and his latest anthology, *A Million Brilliant
Poems – Part One* (A&C Black) was shortlisted for the
coveted Centre for Literacy in Primary Education
Poetry Award 2011.

PURPLE CLASS AND THE SKELINGTON
Sean Taylor
Illustrated by Helen Bate
Cover illustrated by Polly Dunbar

Meet Purple Class: Jamal who keeps forgetting his
book, Jodie with her crazy snake Slinkypants, Ivette
who is best at everything, Leon the rope-swinger,
Yasmin who is sick on every school trip, Shea the
know-all on blood-sucking slugs, and Zina. . .

When Purple Class find a skeleton sitting in
Mr Wellington's chair, what are they going to say
to the school inspector? The adventures of this
calamitous cast of classmates will make you
laugh out loud in delight.

PURPLE CLASS AND THE FLYING SPIDER
Sean Taylor
Illustrated by Helen Bate
Cover illustration by Polly Dunbar

Purple Class are back in four new school stories!
Leon has managed to lose 30 violins, much to
the horror of the violin teacher; Jodie thinks
she has uncovered an unexploded bomb in
the vegetable patch; Shea has allowed Bad Boy,
Purple Class's guinea pig to escape; and Ivette
has discovered a scary flying spider, just in time
for Parent's Evening!

**PURPLE CLASS
AND THE HALF-EATEN SWEATER**
Sean Taylor
Illustrated by Helen Bate
Cover illustration by Polly Dunbar

Mr Wellington's precious cricket sweater is in
the bin, Shea and Jamal have to do a half-hour
sponsored silence, Jodie says there's a werewolf
on the class trip, and Ivette's surprise birthday
cake gets sat on. Four crazy stories about
the funniest class ever.

"Crammed full of zany and exuberant characters
and the mishaps and mayhem that ensue."
Jake Hope, *Achuka*

THE DUMPY PRINCESS
Karin Fernald
Illustrated by Sophie Foster

Princess Victoria lives in a world of dolls, pets
and palaces. But with four bad uncles, a penniless
widowed mother and wicked Sir John Conroy for
company, life isn't easy. It takes Victoria's
down-to-earth governess Lehzen, a nice German
cousin called Albert and her beloved spaniel Dash to
convince the plain little girl with no chin that one day
she could become Queen of England.
A hilarious glimpse into a royal childhood.

'Child-centred history at its most approachable.'
Nicholas Tucker, *The Independent*